JUMP THE CRACKS

Stacy DeKeyser

 JUMP THE CRACKS

Woodbury, Minnesota

First Edition
Third Printing, 2010

Book design by Steffani Sawyer
Cover design by Lisa Novak
Cover image © 2007 Brand X Pictures

Flux, an imprint of Llewellyn Publications

The Cataloging-in-Publication Data for *Jump the Cracks* is on file at the Library of Congress
  ISBN: 978-0-7387-1274-1

Flux
Llewellyn Publications
A Division of Llewellyn Worldwide Ltd.
2143 Wooddale Drive
Woodbury, MN 55125-2989
www.fluxnow.com

Printed in the United States of America

Acknowledgments

Heartfelt thanks to Dori Chaconas, Amanda Jenkins, Kim Marcus, Linda Sue Park, Tanya Lee Stone, and the Wednesday Writers Who Meet on Tuesday, for sharing their time, their wisdom, and their honest feedback.

To Karen Riskin, Tracey Adams, and Josh Adams, for being enthusiastic cheerleaders and awesome agents.

To Andrew Karre, who "got it" from the beginning, who convinced me that Revisions Are Fun, and whose vision, humor, and passion brought out my best.

To the Society of Children's Book Writers and Illustrators, for its generous Work-in-Progress Grant.

To Stephanie, Michaela, and Nicki, for waiting patiently; and to my dad, Nick Chaconas, who told me to finish the book.

Most especially to Kelly, Tom, and Steven for their love and support, without which I could not have written a single word.

To Kelly
of course

ONE

"Do you have your train ticket?"

"Yes, Mother."

"Your emergency money and change for the phone?"

"You saw me put it in my pocket. Besides, I have the cell phone." I waved it in front of her face.

Mom didn't take her eyes off the traffic. "You can't rely on cell phones, Victoria. Keep some change for the pay phone just in case. And that fifty dollars—it's not all for junk food and magazines, you know. It's emergency money. Call me as soon as you get to your father's." She let out a long breath and shook her head. "I still can't believe I'm letting you do this."

"Mom, I'm fifteen. Besides, we made a deal."

"And that credit card is *only* for absolute desperate emergencies, understand? Don't even take it out of your pocket otherwise."

"Okay, I get it! Absolute desperate emergencies only. No problem."

"Maybe we should call Dad just to make sure he has the right time."

"We called him last night. Good grief, Mom. If it means enough to him, he'll be there."

"Honey, please don't be so dramatic. He doesn't love you any less just because he can't come to every school play or softball game. This is hard on him too, you know."

"Yeah. I'm not the one who left."

"Then why are you going, Victoria? No one's forcing you."

"I'm going for decent pizza, and real Chinese, and Saks and Barney's and Bloomie's. Besides, how else can he see exactly how miserable I am?"

"You *will* be miserable if I find out you're spending that kind of money." She sighed. "You know, you're right. You and Dad need to spend some time together. But please, have a good long talk. It'll be good for both of you."

She pulled over to the curb and put the car into park. "I'll have to just drop you off. I'm running late. All you're taking is that little backpack, for a month at your father's?"

"Mom. You worry too much."

"I know it. I can't help it." Then she shrugged and smiled. "Have fun, okay? I'll miss you, baby."

"Oh, Mom." I threw my arms around her and squeezed her tight. "I'll miss you, too."

The Hartford station is a sad little one-track wreck on the escape route to New York. It must have been beautiful a long time ago. On the track side you can see the carved red stone of the building, and the big arched windows all in a row. You'd never know it from the street side, where it's completely covered with this disgusting metal and plastic from the psychedelic sixties. What were they thinking when they did that? Did people go around then, saying, "Hmmm, there's just too much beauty in the world. What can we ugly up today?"

Ten minutes until departure. Enough time to stock up on reading material and breakfast, and to plan my seating strategy. Comfort is very important when you're going to be stuck on a train with strangers for three hours.

I stood in line at the newsstand and separated out the fifty bucks Mom gave me from my own stash of allowance money, and put the Mom money back in my pocket. I'm not totally irresponsible. I know perfectly well the difference between emergency-*emergency* money, and emergency-*there's-a-really-good-sale-at-Bloomingdale's* money. I bought my stuff and then headed up the wide stone steps to the platform.

The train blew into the station with a high-pitched screech of brakes on rails. Just when I was sure my eardrums were going to pop, the train stopped, and the screeching did too.

A hiss of compressed air opened the doors all along the length of the train, one door at either end of each silver car.

I stepped through the front door of the first car and worked my way toward the back of the train, scouting for a decent seat. Kicking aside the crumpled newspapers and empty coffee cups in the aisle, I did my Goldilocks thing: *this* seat has too many crumbs…*this* window has too many schmutzes…the bathroom on *this* car reeks….Good grief, doesn't anyone ever clean these trains?

I finally found an acceptable spot and hurled my backpack onto the bars of the overhead rack. I slid onto the faded blue plush of the aisle seat and dropped my essentials onto the window seat: five gossip magazines and a giant crunch bar. That should get me as far as New Haven, anyway.

There were only a few other people in the car, so I had both seats to myself. Most of the commuters had already taken one of the early trains to New York. The way Dad used to. Before the world blew apart, in more ways than one.

Dad moved out over Labor Day weekend last year. As in, September 2001. I strongly advised against the whole thing. Well, what I said was, "This stinks. Why can't you people figure out how to live together? Don't you care about how I feel?"

They said, "Of course we do, honey."

He left anyway.

His apartment in Chelsea was still full of boxes on September 11. I thought Mom was absolutely going to lose it that day. One minute she's telling Dad good riddance, and practically the next minute she's crying and screaming into the phone trying to find out where he is. Didn't I tell them to try and work it out?

In my former, pre-divorce life, Mom and I took the train into the city practically once a week in the summers, to go shopping and to meet Dad for lunch. I knew the route by heart. But after the divorce, I had to beg for months before they'd let me go on my own. Even though they'd promised me last year. It was part of the deal we made when Dad moved out, as if that would make up for everything else. It didn't, of course. Not by a long shot, but a deal is a deal and I wanted my trip to the city.

Dad finally softened up. He converted his spare room into a bedroom for me.

"It'll be your second home," he said. "Here for you any time you want. How many girls are lucky enough to have their own Manhattan digs?"

Which just made me mad. *Second home?* What the hell does that mean? Home can only be one place. That's what "home" *means.* "Two homes" is like "most unique." Unique means one of a kind, nothing else like it. And just like something is either *unique* or it's not, someplace is either *home* or it's not. Telling me I had two homes just made me feel like I had no home at all.

Mom was ready to nix the whole trip. She said, "The world is a dangerous place, Victoria. Especially New York City." I gave her the comforting argument that a cloud of smallpox will find Farmington, Connecticut, just as easily as New York or anywhere else. Of course I'm scared to be in New York. It's just that I'm not any *less* scared staying home. So why not keep myself occupied with a summer of kick-ass shopping in the city? It could be very therapeutic.

She wasn't buying it.

When logic didn't work, I resorted to guilt. "Does a promise mean nothing to you anymore? Your marriage vows go out the window, so you think you're off the hook for everything else?" She tried to tell me how people can't promise not to change, but I didn't want to hear it. People shouldn't make promises they can't keep.

Maybe the guilt thing worked, or maybe she finally just wanted me out of the house for a while. Either way. She bought me a train ticket.

She also bought me a cell phone and programmed in all of Dad's numbers. Then she made him swear not to be late meeting me at Penn Station. And now here I was, on the train to New York on the first day of summer vacation, with a pocket full of spending money and a pile of trashy magazines to keep my mind off the real world.

I like reading the gossip mags. It's mostly idiotic stuff, but it's fun to read about famous people. If they want to be famous, that's what they get. I like to find out if they're decent or not behind their public faces. It helps me decide what movies to go to, what music to buy, stuff like that. Moral fiber is important. You can have money, or fame, or brains, but if you act like a jerk, then what's the point? Mom was right about one thing. The world *is* a dangerous place. There are people out there trying to kill us all in our beds. Right now you could be inhaling nerve gas, or anthrax, or God knows what. Do you want to take your last breath as a total jerk, or as a decent human being?

As far as I'm concerned, there's no excuse not to be decent.

TWO

Kick.

What the...?

Kick-kick-kick.

Okay. Somewhere between "Stars Who Overeat in Secret" and "Prince William's Favorite Girls' Names," someone *(kick)* decided to occupy the seat behind me *(kick)*. And kick the back of my seat *(kick-kick)*. I vaguely remembered the last stop. This someone *(kick)* must have boarded then. Good grief *(kick)*. And barely ten minutes on the *(kick)* train.

Kick-kick-kick-kick-kick.

I turned around and peeked through the narrow opening between the seats.

There it was. Sitting on the edge of the seat, swinging its feet like that's what made the train go. Legs just long enough to give my seat a good kick with every swing. Dark hair, big brown eyes, runny nose. Then it looked right at me.

"Ha!" it squealed, and it reached forward, grabbing for my eye like it was some kind of toy stuck between the seats. Just then, the train hit a curve and banked left. The kid toppled sideways and disappeared. It started to wail. Oh, yikes. I didn't mean for it to fall and hurt itself.

"What're you doing on the floor? Get up here!" A hand reached down and brought up an arm, then the entire kid, runny nose and all. Now its eyes were wet too. The Hand plopped the kid down on the seat and wiped his nose with a shredded tissue.

"Mama," he whimpered.

"Drink your pop," said The Hand, and it pushed a plastic sippy cup at the kid's chest. He took the cup, sniffled some of his snot, and smiled up at her. Then he leaned forward to look for my eye again.

No way. Time to move to a new neighborhood, before we have more injuries.

I stuck my half-eaten crunch bar in Prince William's face and closed the magazine, gathered up the rest of my junk, and went cruising. As I passed the kid's seat, I couldn't help glancing over.

"Ba!" he said. I guess that meant, "Bring back that eye so I can poke it."

"Go to sleep now," said The Hand.

It turned out that The Hand was attached to a girl not a whole lot older than me. A blue snake tattoo crawled around one side of her neck. Obviously going for the classic beauty look. And sleep? That kid was the untiredest-looking two-year-old I'd ever seen. He just smiled and went on kicking my former seat.

The best I could do was across the aisle and one seat behind them. At least he couldn't kick my seat, and unless he turned around and hung out into the aisle, he wouldn't be able to see me. I just hoped he wouldn't wail all the way to New York.

It was ten o'clock. Time to cruise the café car to see if there was anything good left. They don't always bother to restock their snack inventory after the early runs (God knows they never check the toilet paper supply), so by this time it'd be hit or miss. I decided that if the café car was out of Diet Coke, I'd hop off at the New Haven change-over. That's where the train stops for about ten minutes while they change engines from diesel to electric for the ride into the city. Plenty of time to hit the vending machines. All I needed was the right motivation. I was motivated to get *off* by the thought of peanuts, cookies, and Diet Coke. I was motivated to get back *on* by the thought of having to call Dad from New Haven to tell him my train was on the way to New York without me. Not a pretty thought.

I dug into my pocket and pulled out five singles from my Bloomingdale's money. The train was already slowing down. Time to check out the café car.

"Sit yourself down right now!"

I looked up.

"I told you to go to sleep."

Oh. It was The Hand over across the aisle. The little guy was standing on the seat with his goopy face pressed against the window, coming *this* close to toppling over again with every bump and sway of the train. He pointed against the glass and said, "Da?"

"That ain't no dog. It's a cow. And I told you to sit your butt down!" The Hand grabbed him by one arm again. He looked like a doll, swinging by his arm like that.

Then I saw something I hadn't noticed before.

Around each of the baby's arms, just above the elbow, there was a ring of bruises.

The Hand dropped him onto the seat and tossed a ragged teddy bear at him.

"Da?" he said, pointing toward the window.

"Shut up and go to sleep."

The train lurched to a stop and the doors hissed open. I'd missed my chance for the café car, but that was fine with me. All of a sudden I needed fresh air.

I grabbed my backpack and made for the door.

↔ ↔ ↔

I was off and on again in less than three minutes. I settled in with Diet Coke, cookies, a bottle of water, and an apple. Man does not live on crap alone, you know.

Something was different, though. The seats across the aisle were empty.

Oh, thank God. Those two were really kind of creeping me out.

The train started its slow pull out of the station. As it gained speed and settled into its rock-a-bye rhythm, I melted back into the seat and closed my eyes.

I liked riding the train. Despite the sanitation glitches, Amtrak was not a bad experience—reclining airplane-style seats with tray tables. Air conditioning. The Metro North commuter train was cheaper, but it was a school bus on rails. The blood-red vinyl seats were sticky in the summer and slippery in the winter. The air conditioning was usually broken and the windows were usually stuck shut.

But Metro North had one advantage. It stopped at Grand Central Terminal.

I was six years old the first time I saw Grand Central. The three of us had gotten all dressed up to see the Christmas Spectacular at Radio City Music Hall. We stepped off the train, walked through the tunnel and then—*wow*. The walls and ceiling seemed to fall away, and we were standing in this huge cavernous room. I loved it all instantly —the creamy marble everywhere, the high windows, the gigantic brass clock. The bustle of tourists, commuters, and Christmas shoppers.

But the best part was the ceiling. It was painted to look like the night sky, and I was sure it was as high as the sky itself. Thousands of tiny light bulbs twinkled in the shapes of the constellations. I gripped Dad's hand tight to keep from falling over backward, and he laughed and cradled my head with his free hand.

But a lot has changed since I was six. The Radio City Christmas Spectacular isn't spectacular anymore. I wouldn't be caught dead in a red velvet dress. And now if I want to see Dad I have to go to the city by myself, because he's already there.

Grand Central is as beautiful as ever, though. At least there are some things you can still depend on.

But today I was on Amtrak, and Amtrak goes to Penn Station.

Dad told me that once upon a time, Penn Station had been as grand as Grand Central. But in 1963 it was torn down to make room for Madison Square Garden. I've seen the Garden, and I ask: What kind of tradeoff is that? Was absolutely everyone smoking weed in that decade?

But Dad said that losing the old Penn Station actually saved Grand Central. When people saw what happened, they protested and Grand Central was preserved. That's worth something, I guess.

So now I was headed to ugly Penn instead of beautiful Grand Central. But at least my seat reclined.

Behind me, I heard the door between the cars slide open. I let my eyelids drift up just enough to see through my lashes.

It was The Hand. She hadn't gotten off after all. She'd only gone for provisions, which appeared to be a can of orange soda and a can of beer. But what had she done with the baby? Traded him for a fake ID?

She sat down again across the aisle, popped open the can of beer, and took a good long swig. She let her head fall back against the seat and closed her eyes.

"Pop?" said a voice, and a little hand held up a sippy cup.

I sat up straight.

He'd been there all along. I just hadn't seen him in the window seat. The Hand had left him alone while she went to get herself a beer.

I squirmed and tried to concentrate on "What's in the Stars for the Stars."

But I couldn't. I peeked over the top of the mag and watched.

"I got your pop," said The Hand, taking another swallow of beer.

"Pop?" said the little guy again, shaking his cup and reaching for the can of beer. All I could think of was how hungry he must be to want that orange soda so much. And it looked like that was all he was getting.

The Hand finally opened the soda can. "Give me that," she said, taking the cup.

"Pop," he said, that streaky dirty snotty little face smiling up at The Hand like she'd just given him the sweetest kiss. He drank down the orange soda and started kicking the seat in front of him.

I couldn't move. I just sat there, rubbing my sweaty palms on my jeans and trying not to stare across the aisle.

She'd left him alone in the seat while she walked two cars down to the café car for a beer. While the train was stopped. With the doors wide open and people getting on and off all over the place. And she gave him bruises and she had a fake ID and drank beer at ten in the morning and she had no business being responsible for a little kid. If she hurt him again, I'd—I'd what? Talk sense into her? Give her a stern warning?

No one else seemed to notice what was going on across the aisle. Or maybe they just pretended not to notice. People sat there, reading their newspapers. Chatting. Totally oblivious. How could they not notice?

Maybe when the conductor came by, I could stop him and tell him what had been going on. Or I could go find him now. Or I could hop off in Stamford and find a cop. Or I could hop off in Stamford and stand there, watching the train pull away, and I'd never have to lay eyes on them or think about them ever again. I didn't care how many times Dad would kill me for missing the train.

But I couldn't leave. He was just a baby. If his own mother wouldn't take care of him, who would?

CLUNK!

"Maaaaa-maaaa . . . !"

"What the hell are you doing on the floor? Get up here now!"

There she went again, hauling up the entire kid by his skinny little bruised arm. I rubbed my jeans until I thought they'd light on fire.

He was crying so loud. A pink spot was blooming just above his left eyebrow. He put his hand to his head and cried and cried.

"You hush," she said through her teeth.

The door between the cars slid open and the conductor came breezing through.

Before I had time to think, I stepped into the aisle.

"Excuse me, but there's a problem."

"Problem? Let's see your ticket."

"No, it's not my ticket, my ticket's fine . . . ."

"Victoria Dowling? That's you?"

I nodded. "Yes, but—"

"This is for Penn Station, honey. Two more stops." He handed back my ticket and tried to push past.

"No, wait. I need help," I whispered. "That baby there needs help."

"Huh? Now, I'm sure he's just cranky. All them kids get cranky on the train."

"But she might hurt him. Please. Can you do something?"

"Do something?" He frowned and looked across the aisle.

The Hand was holding Little Guy's head in her hands, inspecting the pink bump.

"They seem okay to me," said the conductor. "I'm sure he's just cranky. Now excuse me, honey. I got work to do." He squeezed past me and kept walking. I glanced over to see if The Hand had overheard us, but she was talking to Little Guy.

"What'm I gonna do with you? You're nothing but a little pain in the ass, you know that?"

The baby sniffled and stared into her eyes. I hoped he didn't understand all the words.

One more hour to Penn Station. If I could just hold on until then, I could tell Dad everything, and he'd know what to do. Only one more hour.

"Maaaaa-maaaa . . . ." wailed Little Guy from across the aisle.

I could feel the muscles in my shoulders tightening. The Hand was curled up in her seat now, trying to sleep.

"Maaaaa-maaaa . . . ."

"Shhh," said The Hand, and she pulled the baby onto her lap. He snuggled into her chest, she kissed the top of his head, and they both were quiet.

Oh, good grief. The conductor was right and I was being ridiculous. Lots of parents blow up at their kids in public—parents a lot older than this one, too. You see it all the time in the grocery store and at the mall. Mom did it plenty of times with me when I was little. When I was big. Last week. Who was I to judge?

I needed to distract myself. I opened my new phone and tried out the camera. I snapped a few pictures . . . of Long Island Sound outside my window . . . of Little Guy, but I mostly got the top of his head and a bit of The Hand's fashionable snake tattoo . . . . I even took a picture of myself by holding the phone at arm's length. It was kind of crooked and it made my nose look big, but otherwise it turned out okay.

I hadn't downloaded any ring tones yet, and I couldn't do it now without annoying everyone. So for the time being

I was stuck with the dumb little *dee-deet* song that you hear a zillion times a day from a zillion different phones.

What was my phone number again? I scrolled through the menus to find it, and then I pulled out a pen and copied the number about ten times on the cover of my magazine, until I had it memorized. Knowing your own cell phone number is important. You never know when that cute guy in homeroom might ask you for it. Or if you had to tell it to someone at 911 because the girl across the aisle was smacking her kid around.

The distractions didn't seem to be working. My eyes were drawn across the aisle like pins to a magnet.

Their seats were empty again. I peeked up and down the aisle.

No one.

I leaned forward for a better view across the aisle.

Nothing.

I tiptoed over to the seats behind theirs, and peeked over the back of the seats.

"Boo!" A head popped up at me.

I jumped and hit my head on the overhead rack.

"Ow! What the hell?" I rubbed my head and opened my eyes.

There we were, standing nose to snotty nose. I could smell his orangey breath, and something else coming from the region of his pants.

"Ha!" he said, and plopped down onto his seat.

"You little…"

"Boo!"

"Stop that! Where's your mother?" I scolded, as if it was his fault she'd taken off again. I still didn't see her anywhere.

"Is she in the bathroom?" I whispered into his face. "Or did she go for another beer?"

"Ha!" he said, and dropped down into the seat again, his butt in the air and his face in the seat cushion.

"Yeah, well. For your information, I can still see you." He was scrunched up in the middle of all the junk she'd left on their seats—his ratty teddy bear, the empty soda and beer cans, and a blue canvas bag, sitting wide open. Inside the bag I could see two diapers, an open carton of cigarettes, and a torn brown paper sack, with—

"Ba!" He popped up, an inch from my face. What was that I saw?

"BOO!" I said back at him, and he squealed and dropped again.

There it was, wrapped with a rubber band and sticking out of the torn paper sack. A big fat stack of cash.

THREE

"All right, that's it. I'm outta here." I hopped over to my own seat and scrunched down next to the window.

And I'd started to feel sorry for her. Couldn't afford to buy her kid anything but orange soda, huh? Yeah, right.

I closed my eyes and tried to sleep away the last twenty minutes.

Then something smacked me on the knee.

"What the … hey!"

"Boo!"

The kid had decided to come over for a visit.

"Bad idea. Terrible idea. Go back to your seat, little boy."

"Up," he said, and he started trying to climb onto the seat next to me.

"No *up*," I whispered. "Go. We'll both get in trouble. Besides, you smell funny."

"Oof—up." His legs pumped the air for a second, and then he was on the seat.

Now he was standing on the seat, looking me right in the eye. He held up his grimy hand and opened and closed his fist about two inches from my face.

"Hi."

"Okay, little boy, this isn't … "

And then I looked at him.

His face was sticky with soda and dried snot. He had a bump above one eyebrow. His juicy orange-stained mouth was full of perfect little white teeth, and his streaky cheeks looked as soft as pillows. His eyes were big and clear and they looked all the way to the back of my brain.

"Hi." He did the hand thing again.

"Hi. You're in big trouble, you know."

"No."

"Very funny. Come on, let's get you back to your seat."

I tried to pick him up, but he made himself all loose and wiggly and he slid right out of my hands.

"No. Book?" He reached under himself and pulled out one of my gossip mags. He pointed at the cover and said, "Da!"

"You like books? That's a horse. And that's Prince William riding him. He's the world's most eligible bachelor. Prince William, not the horse."

"Da," said Little Guy, nodding and turning pages.

"Horse."

"Da?"

"Hor—whatever. Sorry, kid, but this won't work." I got a good grip on him this time and swung him, magazine and all, across the aisle and into his seat. He giggled like he was on a ride at Disneyland.

I couldn't resist peeking into the canvas bag one more time. Sure enough, there it was: a few fat stacks of bills and even some loose hundreds, half-hidden in a crumpled, torn paper bag. How much money was it?

Whatever. I didn't want to be caught anywhere near it.

I hopped to my side of the aisle as quickly as I could. Little Guy stood up and looked at me over the back of his seat, smiling and teetering and doing the hand thing.

"Stay!" I said. As if he were a puppy or something.

The door to the toilet slid open and here came The Hand.

"Ba!" said Little Guy, dropping into his seat.

"Just leave me out of this, kid," I whispered to myself. I grabbed another mag and hid behind it.

"Where'd you get that?" The magazine came flying across the aisle and onto the seat in front of me. No high culture for this girl, no sir.

"Let's go," she said. She stuffed the teddy bear and sippy cup into her canvas bag.

A cell phone rang, *dee-deet.*

Dad. Thank goodness, he was already at Penn Station, waiting for me. I reached for my backpack, but the ringing stopped.

"Yeah. We'll be there in a few minutes."

It was The Hand's phone that had rung.

"We need a place tonight. Yes, I said *we*. I told you that already. I got no choice."

"'Lo?" said Little Guy, reaching for the phone.

The Hand jerked away from him and walked toward the back of the car. While her back was turned, he wiggled down from the seat and crawled across the aisle for the magazine.

"What can I do? He's my kid. You just be there to pick us up!" She smacked the phone shut.

We were underground now. Beneath Manhattan and nearly at Penn Station. It was dark outside the train and bright inside, so everything inside the car was reflected in the windows. I kept my back to her as I watched her reflection walk to her seat and grab the canvas bag. She slung it over her shoulder, then turned to Little Guy across the aisle and pointed to her feet.

"Get—over—here—now."

The baby whimpered. The Hand reached over and grabbed him, dragging him toward her, and he dropped the magazine. She lifted him up by his shoulders and held him close to her face. Her voice stayed low, but not low enough.

"What'm I gonna do with you?" she said, holding him there as if she were waiting for him to answer. They stared into each other's eyes for what seemed like half of forever. Then he opened his mouth and wailed like a siren.

The train lurched and slowed, sending The Hand

staggering backward into her seat. Little Guy landed on top of her, his siren wail as piercing as ever.

Now there was noise and movement everywhere. People stood up, stretched, pulled bags down from the overhead. Newspapers rustled, conversations got louder, but nobody even seemed to notice what was going on right behind them.

I couldn't move.

"Book!" the baby wailed, pointing to the floor and trying to wiggle free. The Hand's phone rang again.

"'Lo?"

"Dammit!" She slid out from under him to answer it, and then she stood up and started walking toward the back of the car.

The baby disappeared under the seats for a few seconds. Then he reappeared with the magazine and plopped it onto the seat. He pointed to the cover and said, "Orse." Then he looked right up at me and smiled.

"Shhh!" I whispered, trying not to look at him. I pulled my backpack down from the overhead rack. "Hey. Did you say—?"

"What? You be there, you hear me? I'm not sleeping on the street tonight!" The Hand paced back in my direction. I opened my backpack and pretended to pack while I watched out of the corner of my eye. The baby kept turning pages and pointing at different pictures.

"You listen, Jake," said The Hand, lowering her voice. "I got your stuff, so you come get it. Don't you threaten..." She stopped pacing and her face turned pale. She looked down at Little Guy. Then she slowly shut her cell phone and sank into her seat.

"Orse," said Little Guy to The Hand, pointing at the magazine.

She just sat there for a few seconds. Then she held her hand out to Little Guy.

"Let me see that."

He gave her the magazine, and she flipped through it briefly.

Then The Hand looked up. I jerked my head down and hoped she hadn't seen me watching her in the window's reflection.

She rolled the magazine into a tight tube, shoved it into her canvas bag, and stood up. "Come on." She grabbed the baby's arm with her free hand, and pulled him toward the back of the car.

"Orse! Orse!" cried the baby, reaching for the canvas bag.

"Shh! Shut up!"

"Book!" The baby went all loose and wiggly again, but she held on tight and dragged him down the aisle by his arm. Then she opened the door to the bathroom.

"Wait!" I yelled, dropping my backpack onto the seat and stumbling toward them. I didn't know what I was doing, but I couldn't stand the thought of them alone in the locked bathroom.

Then our eyes met for the first time.

I forced myself not to flinch or look away. I stared straight into her face and saw defiance and anger. But there was something else there, too. What was it? Whatever it was, it gave me the guts to keep moving.

"I ... I left something in the bathroom ... let me get it quick."

I pushed past her and into the toilet, sliding the door shut with a bang.

If I stayed in there long enough, she'd either have to calm down in front of all those people in the train car, or she'd have plenty of witnesses watching her pound on her kid. But the stink of heavily used and rarely cleaned lavatory hit me full in the face. I wouldn't last more than thirty seconds in here. The smell combined with the motion of the slowing train made me dizzy. Suddenly all I wanted was to get off the damn train.

"Hey! Hurry up in there!"

I splashed my face in the dribble of cold water at the tiny sink and opened the door. I tried to squeeze past without looking at them. But someone was blocking my way.

The Hand was staring at me again. I froze, and my eyes locked on hers for a second time. She took a step closer, until her face was just inches from mine.

"You," she whispered. "Be careful."

Then she stepped past me into the bathroom and pulled Little Guy inside, sliding the door shut behind them.

I stood there for a second, my mind trying to absorb the threat. Then I shook it off. I wasn't afraid for myself. I was afraid for Little Guy.

I put my ear to the door, but I couldn't hear anything

above the usual train noises. I stumbled back to my seat to grab my stuff, never taking my eyes off that bathroom door. The train was moving at a slow grind, and in the dark outside I could see networks of tracks, and other trains, and more lights. We were pulling into Penn Station.

People were staggering down the aisle now, elbowing their way to the back of the car to wait at the doors. I crammed my stuff into my backpack and zipped it shut, still watching the bathroom door.

Finally the door opened and she stepped out. I wasn't sure at first, because there were so many people crowding in the aisle. But I watched for a few seconds and then I knew for sure.

She was alone.

FOUR

She yanked the door shut behind her and fought her way through the people standing in the aisle. I turned my back and watched her reflection in the windows. She was definitely alone. She pushed through the aisle—toward the front of the car.

I looked back at the bathroom door, and then toward the front of the car. Maybe she was getting a suitcase, or a stroller, or something else big that she'd stowed up front in the baggage cubby. But I'd already lost her in the bunch of people crowded at the front door. Just then, the train lurched to a stop with that earsplitting squeal, and the doors hissed open. I watched for her as everyone pushed down the steps and out the door. After a minute the crowd cleared and the front of the car was empty.

She was gone.

I dove to the window and tried to find her in the crush of people on the platform. Finally, I spotted her—leaning against a column while the crowd streamed around her on their way to the escalators and the exits. No stroller. No suitcase. No Little Guy. She glanced at her watch, hitched her canvas bag up on her shoulder, and headed toward the escalators with everyone else.

The train emptied out quickly. I stumbled to the back of the car and stood in front of the bathroom door.

I put my ear to the door. Nothing.

I tried the knob. It wasn't locked, so I turned it and slid the door open.

There he was, pulling paper towels out of the trash bin like he was on a treasure hunt. He looked up and smiled.

"Hi."

"Oh, God. You scared the hell out of me."

"Book?" He held out his hand.

"Your mom took it. Come on, you can't stay here." I picked him up, pulled a paper towel out of his fist, and stepped out of the bathroom.

I stood with him at the top of the steps so I could have a better view of the platform, but I didn't see Dad anywhere. And I didn't see a conductor, and I didn't see The Hand.

"Okay, relax," I told myself. "It's crowded. Dad's here somewhere."

I stood there, waiting for the crowd to clear, and hoping that even if I couldn't see Dad, he would see me.

After a minute or so, the crowd thinned. But no Dad.

"Oh, come on," I said out loud. "Where are you?"

"Down?" said Little Guy, wiggling.

"Not yet." I hoped he wouldn't slip out of my hands, which were starting to get sweaty. "He'll be here any second. He promised."

I waited a second. Ten seconds. Sixty seconds. But he wasn't there.

"Down!" Little Guy squirmed harder, until I almost lost my grip on him. I had to grab a strap of his overalls with one hand and pull him back up until he sat on my other arm. He was not happy about it.

"Soon, okay?" I scanned the platform again for Dad.

Nothing.

"Of all times to be late. This is the most unbelievable thing in the whole wide stinking world."

And even though most of me knew that Dad was probably stuck in Seventh Avenue traffic, one tiny little piece of me repeated those words I'd told Mom—*If it means enough to him, he'll be there.*

Maybe it *didn't* mean enough to him.

It wouldn't be the first time something like this had happened.

It was the bottom of the seventh in the final game of last summer's disastrous softball season, and we were down by a run. I was due to bat second in the inning, which meant that for once (thank God) I wouldn't make the last out of the game.

I scanned the bleachers from the on-deck circle. Mom was there with a bunch of other parents, smiling and wiggling her fingers at me. But no Dad.

I knew it'd be a tight squeeze for him. But I also knew that if he could catch the early train home from New York, and then break a traffic rule here or there on the drive from the Hartford station, he could make it by the third inning.

But now we were down to our last outs, and I knew one more thing: If he wasn't here by now, he wasn't coming at all.

I don't care, I thought to myself. *It's his loss.*

But I did care. I wanted to run all the way to New York and scream at him.

Long story short: The leadoff batter walked, I stepped to the plate, swung at the first pitch, and smacked it over the fence. Game over. We win, 2-1.

The whole team was waiting for me at home plate to smother me with hugs and high-fives. My first-ever home run, and a game-winner no less. It was awesome.

I looked up from the pile, and there was Mom, on her feet, holding her cell phone over her head. She motioned for me to come over to the bleachers.

I knew who was on the phone.

I turned my back and walked to the dugout, sur-
rounded by my cheering teammates.

↔ ↔ ↔

"Don't be ridiculous," I said, taking a deep breath. "This
is Penn Station, not a stupid softball game. He'll be here.
Let's go to Plan B."

"Bee?"

I looked at Little Guy, and vaguely wondered how he
ended up in my arms.

"Yeah, Plan B." And I explained it to him, even though
I knew he didn't get it. But saying it out loud made me feel
a little more in control of things. "If I don't see Dad when
I get off the train, I'm supposed to go upstairs and stand
under that big board that lists all the trains and times and
stuff. Then I'm supposed to call him. That's probably
where I ought to take you, anyway. To a policeman, or
Lost and Found, or something. And then I'm gonna let
Dad have it when he does show up."

I started down the steps of the train.

"Hey! Watch it!"

It was a guy—a huge guy. He was thick and tall, walking fast alongside the train, and steaming mad. He was
on the hunt for someone, and he didn't seem to care how
many people he knocked over in the process. He walked
past me and I smelled sweat and cigarette smoke, even
from the top step. I couldn't take my eyes off him. It was
like watching one of those nature shows where a lion is

stalking zebras. You know something ugly has to happen soon, but you watch anyway.

He must have seen the person he was looking for, because suddenly he stopped and yelled "Hey!" He broke into a run along the narrow platform, pushing people aside as he went. Finally, at the base of the escalator, he stopped and grabbed someone's arm and turned her around—it was The Hand.

So this must be Jake.

He was twice her size and twice as loud. They argued, but I couldn't make out the words. Then Jake yanked the canvas bag away from her and rummaged through it. He pulled out the paper sack, turned it upside down, and shook it. Empty. He tossed it aside, and then he flipped the canvas bag over, letting everything spill out onto the platform. He shuffled his foot through it all, and then kicked it, sending diapers and teddy bear flying. He threw the empty canvas bag on top of the pile.

The Hand crawled around on her hands and knees, gathering everything back into the bag. A few people hesitated as they walked by, as if they thought about helping her, but one look at Jake and they kept walking.

Finally The Hand stood up and turned toward the escalator, but he stepped in front of her and blocked her path. She might as well have been walking into a wall. He grabbed her arm and started walking her away from the escalator and back toward the train. Toward me and Little Guy. Were they coming back to get him?

Suddenly I realized what I'd seen in her eyes earlier, because now I felt it myself.

They were getting closer.

My heart felt like it would pound right through my chest. I backed through the inner door of the train car, praying they wouldn't get on the train too. I took a step up the aisle until I could peek out the window. They were still on the platform, and he still had a tight grip on her arm.

"Where is it?" I heard him say.

The money. That's what he was coming back for. I did a quick check of all the pockets in Little Guy's bib overalls. Nothing but a few dirty tissues.

"Wait a minute," said The Hand. "It must be here somewhere." She shook free of him, opened her canvas bag and started digging through it. Then she glanced up at the train. For a second I thought she looked right at me.

"It's not in there," said Jake. "Get back on that train and find it."

I gasped and turned to make an escape at the other end of the train car. But just as we got to the door, it hissed shut, and I felt the floor jerk underneath me.

The train was moving.

FIVE

"No! This can't be happening!"

But it was happening. I could feel the train slowly picking up speed, and carrying us along with it.

"Holy crap," I whispered. "I can't be on this train! Are *they* on the train? Oh, holy *crap!*"

"Crap?" said Little Guy.

"What? Don't—Oh, come on!"

I reached for the door and yanked on it. It was shut tight—probably locked automatically when the train started moving.

"No—Don't do this. Don't *do this!*" I shook the handle until the door rattled, and then gave it a good hard kick.

I looked around frantically, found the emergency brake cord, and reached for it.

But my eye caught movement outside the window. Jake and The Hand were still on the platform, still arguing. And they were sliding out of view.

My hand dropped to my side.

Okay, so we were trapped in a tin can heading out of town. But I felt suddenly relieved to be safe from Jake and The Hand, even for a little while. Besides, whenever a train leaves New York, another one has to be going back, right? And then, since I could finally breathe and think a little better, something else occurred to me.

"Let's see if she really did leave it on the train somewhere," I said to Little Guy. "Just out of curiosity."

I shifted him on my hip and walked through to the next car, where we'd been sitting before. We looked in the bathroom first, which was totally disgusting but totally empty except for scraps of TP and paper towels scattered on the floor. I held my breath and plunged my arm into the trash bin, feeling around for something kind of solid. But nothing. I washed my hands and arms up to my elbows and looked around. We were in a windowless, gray, smelly little cubicle. There was not a single place to hide anything. Then I heard a flush.

"Down!" said Little Guy. He pushed on the flusher handle again and again, and giggled, reaching into the toilet bowl.

"Hey!" I said, pulling his arm out. "That's so disgusting!"

"Down," he said again, pointing to the toilet.

"Please don't tell me the money's in the toilet." I was pretty sure no amount of money was worth pulling out of the can. But when I looked, I saw "down." Whenever Little Guy flushed, a little trickle of blue disinfectant swirled around inside the toilet bowl, and then a hole opened at the bottom. The blue liquid dribbled out the hole into open air, splattering onto the tracks and the rocks and the weeds two feet below.

Little Guy and I looked at each other.

"Do you think she flushed it onto the tracks?"

"Tracks?" he answered.

"Who knows," I said. "Let's wash your hands."

A minute later, we walked up the aisle to where The Hand and Little Guy had been sitting. Now a woman in a suit was sitting there, reading a newspaper.

"Excuse me," I said to her. "I...we were sitting here earlier, and I think maybe I left something."

"Oh?" She put down her newspaper and smiled at Little Guy. "Have a look around. Let me get up."

"No, that's okay, it'll just take a second." I set Little Guy down and knelt in the aisle, scanning the floor under the seats. I figured it would be pretty easy to spot a naked stack of cash. But there was nothing under the seats. Maybe someone else had already found it.

"There's only the train magazine in the seat pockets," offered the lady.

"I guess it's not here." I straightened up and took Little Guy's hand. "Thanks anyway."

"No problem," she said. "I hope it wasn't anything important."

"Oh, no," I said casually. "No big deal."

Only a gazillion dollars in cash. But it was gone—down the toilet and onto the tracks, in someone else's pocket, or just plain lost. Whatever. It wasn't mine, and it wasn't my problem. My problem was getting back to New York.

"Excuse me again," I said to the lady with the newspaper. "What's the next stop?"

"Newark," she said. "We'll be there in about twenty minutes." Then she got a funny look on her face. She leaned toward me and lowered her voice. "Honey, I think the baby needs a change."

"Change? Oh, sorry. Thanks."

She was right. Little Guy was smelling pretty ripe.

"Okay, here's the deal," I whispered to him as we found a seat. "We'll get off in Newark and get on the first train that's going back to Penn Station. Then we can find a policeman. And a clean diaper. You'll just have to stink until then."

"Stink," agreed Little Guy.

A phone rang.

"'Lo?" said Little Guy.

This time it was my cell phone. I dug it out of my pack and glanced at the caller ID, but I knew it was Dad.

"Yeah, great," I said to myself. "Now he shows up."

I hit the *talk* button.

"Dad?"

"Hi, honey," he said, all out of breath.

"Where *were* you?" I said, fighting to keep my voice low so people wouldn't stare at me. "I waited for you. I looked everywhere for you. You promised—"

"Honey, I'm so sorry. I got held up. Couldn't find a cab to save my life. Don't tell your Mom about this, all right?" he said with a nervous laugh.

It'd serve him right. But I said, "I won't tell Mom about you being late if you don't tell her about me missing my stop in New York."

"I'm heading into the station right now. Meet me at the—what? You missed your stop? Where are you now?"

"I'm still on the train."

"Victoria, how on earth did you manage that?" he said. "Well, I guess now we're even. Just—get off at the next stop, and then get on the first train coming back here. I'll check the schedule and meet you when you get here. It might take an hour or so. I'd better call your mother and tell her everything's under control, so she doesn't worry."

I almost said, "Good idea. *You* lie to her." But what I really said was, "Sure, Dad."

"Okay, sweetie. I'd better call Mom now. I'll be waiting for you."

"Dad, listen—"

But he'd hung up already.

I pushed the *end* button.

"'Lo?" Little Guy said again, reaching for the phone.

"Here. Go nuts." I handed the dead phone over to him. "Can you believe that? He shows up late, and then he cuts me off. He was so scared of getting in trouble with Mom that he didn't even wait to listen to me."

"'Lo? Tee? Hi! Hi, Tee. 'Bye!" He handed the phone back to me with a satisfied look on his face.

"How's everything with Tee?"

"Tee," he said, nodding.

"Good."

Would it really take an hour to get back? Little Guy was really stinking up the place. "Maybe they sell diapers at the newsstand in Newark," I said.

Little Guy. Kid. I didn't know what to call him. I'd never heard The Hand say his name. Not even once.

"Hey, little boy—funny little smelly little kid—what's your name?"

"Name?"

"Yeah. What's your name?"

"No."

"Very funny. Come here and let me see if you have any ID on you."

I pulled him onto my lap for an inspection. No name written on his shirt tag. Nothing on his overall tag. Nothing inside his shoes. I wasn't digging any deeper until I had a clean diaper on me.

"Well, apparently your name is Anonymous." I looked down at him, at his sticky hair and face, and those dark, bottomless eyes. He blinked slowly, gave my chest a vigorous rub with his nose, and closed his eyes.

"Thanks for the souvenir," I whispered. "But what

should I call you? Would it be okay if I give you a name? Just temporarily?"

He was all warm in my arms, and his head was heavy on my chest. It felt nice.

Then I smiled, remembering his new word earlier— "horse," when he was pointing at the pictures of Prince William in the gossip mag. Cute kid. Smart kid.

"William!" I said, and he startled a bit, but didn't wake up.

"Sorry. How about if I call you William? Just for now? That's a nice name. William, the handsome prince."

The handsome prince snuffled into my shirt again.

I laid my cheek on the top of his head. I could feel him breathing, slow, deep, and even. I felt my own body relaxing, and the motion of the train rocked us from side to side. Then I started singing a song I hadn't thought about since I was a little kid. Mom would sing it to me when I was sleepy and the world was safe. She'd comb my hair with her fingers and lean close, smelling of mint from her toothpaste and fresh earth from her garden. I used to think she'd made up the song herself, and that every word was just for me.

You are my sunshine
My only sunshine
You make me happy
When skies are gray.
You'll never know, dear
How much I love you.
Please don't take my sunshine away.

It's amazing how, when you're little, a few simple words and a sweet tune can mean so many things. Love. Security. Trust.

But my mom didn't make up that song. It's an old song that everybody knows. I closed my eyes and tried to remember when I'd figured that out.

And when did I figure out that my parents didn't know the answer to every question? That they couldn't protect me from everything, no matter how much they loved me? Sometimes—lots of times, lately—I wished I could feel the way I did when I was small and the only thing I needed to feel absolutely safe and perfect was my mother, stroking my hair and singing a silly little song.

William's nap only lasted a few minutes. I didn't think it would be a good idea to miss my stop a second time.

The Newark station was a lot smaller than Penn, thank goodness. "Let's go find out which train we need and if we have time to find a diaper," I said. William blinked up at me and smiled.

I showed my ticket to the guy behind the window.

"I missed my stop. Which train goes back to New York?"

"If you want to use this Amtrak ticket here, that'll be goin' out on Track 2," said the ticket guy. "Next train at three o'clock."

"Three o'clock? But it's not even one o'clock now. I can't wait until three o'clock."

"Well, now, you could take the New Jersey Transit line. There's a train into the city every hour, but you'd have to buy a different ticket. If you hurry, you can catch the next one. It's gettin' ready to leave from Track 3 in just a minute. Gets into Penn Station at 1:17."

"Perfect. How much?" I dug a crumpled handful of bills out of my pocket and dumped them on the counter.

"Do you want one way, round trip, or off-peak Super Saver?"

"What? Just one way. Please—I have to make this train!"

"That'll be $3.30. Your little brother there rides free."

The ticket guy picked out a five-dollar bill, punched some buttons, and handed me my ticket and my change.

"Thanks." I grabbed it all with one hand, bounced William higher on my hip, and took off for Track 3.

Dee-deet.

My phone.

"'Lo?"

"Oh, good grief."

It had to be Dad. He probably found out about the three o'clock train too. But I couldn't dig out my phone without putting William down first, and if I did that, I might miss the train. I'd have to wait and call him back once we were on board. I kept running.

Dee-deet.

"'Lo? 'Lo! Tee?" said William, squirming. My backpack slid off my shoulder and bumped against my thigh as I ran. Then Wills kicked. Hard.

"Ow!"

Dee-deet.

"'Lo?"

"Crap!" I had to stop and set him down before I completely lost my grip, and then my backpack slid all the way down my arm and I dropped my train ticket and loose change all over the floor.

I looked up in time to see a train pull away on Track 3.

"Well, isn't this just great."

"'Lo?"

But the phone had stopped ringing.

I glared at Wills. "You kicked me!"

"'Lo!"

"Oh, please. The phone's not always for you."

I checked the caller ID and sure enough, it'd been Dad. But there was no point in calling him back until I knew when the next train was. Besides, a tiny malicious part of me was glad that now *he* was the one waiting for *me*.

I studied the schedule board.

"Great. The next train isn't until 1:57. That's practically another hour." I reached for my phone.

"Pop!" said William.

"What?" I asked, still studying the schedule board. When I looked down, he was already halfway across the waiting room.

"Hey, wait!" I yelled. I bent down, grabbed the train ticket and paper money, left the coins, and took off after William. I caught up to him in front of a soda machine and picked him up, my heart pounding as if I'd just run twenty miles instead of twenty feet.

"You're a handful and a half, aren't you? Now listen,

you can't go running off like that. You scared me half to death."

"Pop," he said again, reaching for the machine.

"Are you thirsty? I bet you're hungry too. Now that you mention it, I'm starving. Let's see if we can find some healthier junk food."

We walked over to the newsstand. I pulled two little cartons of chocolate milk from the cooler, and found two packages of peanut butter crackers, and set it all on the counter.

"Do you have any diapers?" I asked the clerk.

"Not here, honey. There's a little vending machine in the ladies' room where you can buy 'em one at a time, but that's prob'ly empty. You could try the drugstore across the street."

"Thanks."

There was no vending machine in the ladies' room. Well, there used to be something on the wall, but it had been yanked off ages ago. By now William was positively reeking, plus he was getting pretty squishy. But I had to call Dad before I forgot.

This would be fun.

SIX

"Well, the good news is, Dad didn't quite kill me through the phone when I told him I missed the one o'clock train. He mostly just complained about some meeting he's going to miss at the office. The bad news is—I still didn't tell him about you."

"Eat?" said Wills, reaching for the package of peanut butter crackers.

I sighed. Maybe it was better this way. There was nothing Dad could do until we got there, anyway, except worry. And maybe call Mom and tell her, and then I'd never get to come to New York on my own again, or do anything fun for the rest of my life. Despite the divorce, they were still good at ganging up on me when they felt like it.

I handed Wills a cracker. He bit into it, and then started sucking the peanut butter out of the middle of the sandwich.

"That's totally disgusting."

"Mmfg?" He pushed the soggy cracker against my lips.

"No thanks." I wrinkled my nose at him, and he giggled.

"Come on, let's take a walk to the drugstore."

↔ ↔ ↔

Newborn … Small … Medium … Large … Extra-Large … Toddler ….

"Yikes. Well, I think we can eliminate 'newborn.' I'd call you small-to-medium, but in diaper terms, you're apparently gigantic. Do you weigh between 22 and 37 pounds?"

"No."

"These packages are so huge. Do we really need so many diapers?"

All of a sudden, about a zillion containers of baby powder tumbled to the floor. Wills sat in the middle of it all, looking guilty.

"Do you mind?" I whispered, glancing around to see if anyone had noticed. "Come on, put 'em back."

Wills handed me the baby powder containers one by one, and I restacked them on the shelf.

"As I was saying—a handful and a half. I should call you H.H."

"Aych!" he yelled, and bolted down the aisle.

I dropped my shopping basket and chased after him, grabbing him by the overall straps.

"Listen, you little wild man. You have to stop running off like that, or I'll take you to the puppy aisle and get a leash."

"Leash!" he said.

"Oh, good grief."

I steered him back to where I'd dropped the shopping basket. And I kept a grip on his overalls.

"Okay, what else? Do we need any of this other stuff?" I tossed one of the containers of powder into our basket, along with a travel-size packet of baby wipes. I wasn't about to go into this battle unarmed.

"Okay, my stinky prince. Let's go." I picked him up so he couldn't escape again and walked to the checkout.

A radio behind the counter was yacking away on an all-news station.

… *Sunny and warm today, with a high near 80. A perfect day for being outside* …

"Yeah, thanks. Hear that, Wills? We should be having a picnic in Central Park right now, instead of soaking up the smells of Newark."

"Sounds good to me," agreed the lady behind the counter. "That'll be $15.57."

"Fifteen dollars? Uh … do these diapers come in smaller packages?"

"Sorry. I guess the diaper companies figure you'll use 'em up soon enough."

I looked at William. "I'm spending fifteen bucks of my Bloomingdale's money on you."

He gave me a peanut butter kiss.

"Ain't that the sweetest thing?" said the lady. "I'd say that's worth a whole shopping spree at Bloomingdale's."

How could I argue with her? I wrinkled my nose for him again, and he giggled, right on cue.

"You want this all in one bag, miss?"

…In local news, NYPD is investigating the report of a midtown kidnapping…

"Miss? All in one bag?"

"Oh. Sure. Thanks." I slipped my backpack over both shoulders, then I shifted William onto one arm and hung the plastic shopping bag on my other arm. I pushed the door open with my shoulder.

…occurred early this afternoon in Penn Station. Police are reviewing surveillance video taken on the platform and hope to release a photo of the suspect…

I stifled a gasp. The bell at the top of the door jangled, and the clerk glanced up, but her face didn't register anything except boredom. I smiled weakly and left.

My heart pounded and my legs felt wobbly as I stumbled across the street and back toward the station. I held William tight and started thinking out loud.

"Kidnapping? In Penn Station? It must be a coincidence."

But it was too much of a coincidence to be a coincidence.

The Hand must have called the police. Maybe she'd changed her mind, and now she wanted William back, but she was too scared to admit she left him alone on the train, so she claimed that he'd been kidnapped.

And there was surveillance video.

"This whole thing is ridiculous!" I said out loud, kicking open the door of the train station ladies' room. It hit the inner wall with a bang. "You haven't been kidnapped. She *left* you. She *abandoned* you. I'd like to see *that* on the surveillance video. Kidnapped, my ass."

But no matter what the truth was, if Wills *had* been reported kidnapped, the video would also prove that the kidnapper was—me.

"Oh, please!" The words echoed around the dim, tiled room.

Kidnapped.

It sounded so awful. So … criminal. And yet—technically speaking, anyway—it was true.

"What was I supposed to do? Leave you there and forget about you? I didn't plan on still being on the train when it started moving again. It was just an accident. That's not kidnapping."

Or is it? How would I explain it to anyone who wasn't there?

"Is this your baby, miss? Your little brother? Cousin? Neighbor?"

"No … "

"Ever see him before today?"

"Well, no…"

"Did you have permission to take him, miss? Permission from his mother?"

"Well, no…"

"Did you leave the area with him, miss? On a train bound out-of-state, as a matter of fact?"

"Well…"

"There you have it, then. Textbook kidnapping if I ever heard the word. Did I mention we have video?"

Can they put you in jail if you're only fifteen?

"We have to get you back there. That's the only way to prove you weren't actually kidnapped. I was just trying to help you."

"Help you?" he said, rubbing peanut butter into my hair. Suddenly he was all blurry.

"Cut it out," I said, blinking hard. "Come on, let's clean you up. We'll show them I couldn't possibly have kidnapped you. I'm taking care of you. I bought you diapers."

↔ ↔ ↔

I held my breath and chucked the old diaper into the trash bin. It weighed about fifty pounds.

"I have to call Dad again. He can at least tell somebody that you're okay."

I grabbed a layer of wipes about an inch thick and dabbed William's behind.

"But will he let me explain what happened, and will he understand? Or will he freak out?"

I poofed a thick layer of powder on William to cover up the stink that didn't quite want to go away. When he was all put back together, I stood him on the floor and held out my hand. He took it like he'd known me forever.

He trusted me.

Of course, he was only two years old and probably would've trusted an ax murderer with a gentle voice and a supply of peanut butter crackers. All the more reason he needed someone he could really depend on.

I knew how he felt.

"Don't worry," I told him. "Everything's under control. We'll tell the police what happened, and show them your bruises, and they'll help you. I promise. And I always keep my promises."

He blinked at me with his bottomless eyes and nodded.

I rinsed a fresh baby wipe with warm water and washed William's face and hands.

"Wow!" I tried to smile. "There's a cute kid under there after all. Wait a minute…"

I dug my hairbrush out of my pack and gently worked it through his hair until it was smooth and soft as fluff.

Combed hair. Clean face and hands. A cloud of baby powder hanging in the air around him. He was—truly and absolutely—beautiful. And so small.

And in big trouble.

We were both in trouble. Way over our heads in trouble.

"Daddy, help," I whispered, and then I lost it. "Why couldn't you just *be* there when I got off the train? None of this would have happened if you'd just been there like you promised!"

And the room got all blurry again and I sat down on the floor in a heap.

"You're never there for me any more! You *are* supposed to come to my softball games! I finally got to pitch this season! I threw a six-hitter, and you missed it! And now I'm a—" I threw my hairbrush across the bathroom. It bounced off the tile wall with a loud echoing *crack* and fell to the floor in two pieces.

William jumped, and his eyes got big, and then he started to cry too.

"I'm sorry! I'm sorry," I said, and I scooped him up and held him close and rocked him, right there on the ladies' room floor, in the train station somewhere in Newark.

The door squeaked, and two old ladies shuffled in.

"Is everything all right, dear?" one of them said.

I wiped my face with the bottom of my shirt and stood up. "Yeah, we're okay," I mumbled. "Thanks."

I blew my nose on a paper towel. I picked up the pieces of my hairbrush.

"Come on," I whispered to Wills, sniffing hard. "We'd better call Dad from the platform, so we don't miss another train."

I dug my cell phone out of my pack and shoved it into

my back pocket. I tied the bag of diapers onto my backpack by the handles, and slung my pack over both shoulders.

Then I picked up Wills and headed out to catch the 1:57 train.

SEVEN

"Hello?"

I was so relieved to hear his voice, I almost didn't care about being mad at him. I shifted William on my hip.

"Dad? It's me."

"Hi, honey. Where are you? Are you finally on the train?"

"It'll be here any minute. I'm waiting on the platform. Dad, listen—"

"'Lo?" said Wills, reaching for the phone. I made a stern face and shook my head.

"Thank goodness," said Dad. "I've been getting nervous. Do you know that a child disappeared from the station here just a little while ago? A kid who was on the train from Hart-ford."

So he *did* know about the kidnapping. But he didn't say anything about a surveillance video. Maybe it hadn't been broadcast yet.

"Uh … you don't think I'm the missing kid, do you, Dad?"

The actual missing kid pouted because he couldn't have the phone.

"Oh, no," Dad said. "A little boy is missing, a toddler. But it still makes me nervous. A kid any age could just disappear, you know, and never be seen again … "

"I didn't disappear, Dad. I'm right here in Newark, and I'll be on the train in just a minute." I took a deep breath. "Dad, listen. I need to tell you something, but you have to promise not to get mad at me."

"Why?" he said. "What happened?"

"'Lo!" said Wills, giving my head a little whack.

"Not now," I whispered to him.

"Victoria? Who are you talking to?"

"You have to promise me, Dad. I don't know what to do, and I might be in big trouble, but you have to promise not to get mad and you have to promise to help."

There was silence on the other end for a second.

"Okay, now I *am* worried. What's going on, Victoria?"

"Promise, Dad. You have to swear on your life. This is important."

"Honey, I'm your father. I love you. You know I'll do

whatever I can. Now would you please tell me what's going on?"

I tried to breathe evenly, which was hard because suddenly I felt like my chest was being squeezed in a vise.

"Okay, I'm not absolutely sure…"

"'Lo? 'Lo Tee?"

"Victoria, who is that?"

"I'm trying to tell you, Dad. I'm pretty sure…" I didn't know how to say the words, so I just let them spill out. "I mean—I know where that missing kid is." I swallowed hard. "He's with me."

I mostly heard a bunch of sputtering on the other end. "Wha—? Is that who I hear? The missing—?"

"'Lo!"

"Yeah, that's him. He loves talking on the phone. Dad, can you let the police know that Wills is here, and that he's okay, and we're coming back on the 1:57 train? I didn't take him on purpose. It was a huge mix-up. Everything happened so fast. I was so scared for him…."

"Okay," he said, "Okay, calm down." It sounded like he was telling himself as much as he was telling me. "I'm sure there's a good explanation. The important thing is that you're both all right. You're both all right, aren't you?"

"Yes, Dad, we're fine."

"Okay, we'll sort everything out. Just get back here as soon as you can. You have to get that kid back here! Do you want me to come get you?"

"No, Dad. The train will be here any second. We'll be back in New York in a little while."

"All right. But *don't* miss that train, young lady. I'll take care of things on this end. I'll be waiting for you. Everything will be okay."

The tightness in my chest eased up a little. "Thanks, Dad." I wished that train would show up.

"Imagine how his family must feel," said Dad. "That little boy's mother must be frantic with worry. Maybe she's still here somewhere ... "

"What? Dad, no! You don't understand—"

"I'll take care of everything. I'll find a police officer, and we'll have that baby back in his mama's arms in no time. Don't worry, honey. You just get yourselves on that train."

And he hung up.

My hand dropped to my side. "Can you believe it? He promised to help, but he didn't even listen. And now he's going to do exactly the opposite of what we need him to do."

"'Lo! Tee!" said Wills, kicking me.

I handed him the phone. I stared down the empty track, holding tight onto William and singing softly in his ear.

You are my sunshine
My only sunshine ...

"Shine ... " He sang into the phone. I held him close and I rocked him back and forth, until he started to relax and get even heavier in my arms.

You make me happy
When skies are gray ...

"Gray ... " he sang, and his head rolled onto my shoulder. I gently took the phone, then I rocked him and sang to him, and I didn't even notice the train pull in until its brakes squealed and made me jump.

I blinked hard and tried to concentrate. I watched the doors on all the cars slide open, all at the same time, up and down the length of the train. I stood there and rocked William as people got on and off.

"I didn't even get a chance to explain," I whispered. "He promised to help, but he wouldn't even listen. And the minute we get there, they'll take you away from me and give you back to her, and she'll just ... "

You'll never know, dear
How much I love you
Please don't—

I kept rocking Wills and staring at the train, trying to decide what to do. I knew I only had a few seconds before my decision would be made for me.

I counted, and sure enough, thirty-two seconds later, the doors on all the cars slid shut, all at the same time, up and down the length of the train.

And then the train pulled away.

E I GHT

For a minute I couldn't move. Then I took a long breath and buried my face in William's hair. He smelled so wonderful—baby powder, old stink, the whole package. My arms ached, my back ached, but I couldn't put him down. I stood on the platform with him sleeping on my shoulder, trying not to panic and wondering how today had ever happened.

There'd be another train. There was always another train. Right now, I needed time to think.

Dad was being no help at all. He said he'd be there when the train first got into Penn Station, but then he wasn't. He said he'd help when I tried to tell him on the phone what was going on, but then he didn't. Just like he said he still loved me and promised to come back to Connecticut for important stuff, but he hardly ever did. I know it's a long haul up from the city, but he shouldn't say he'll do something and then not do it. I'm not claiming that he actually lied about all those things. He just keeps flaking out, which really isn't any better, because either way, guess who ends up getting screwed?

Well, I wouldn't flake out on Wills. This was important. Wills was in real danger if he went back to The Hand. All I had to do was look at the bruises on his arms to remember that.

I found a bench and gently settled Wills onto my lap.

It had all happened so fast.

Even if I explained everything to the police, that wouldn't guarantee that Wills would be safe. I had no real proof. Bruises can come from anywhere. Besides, why would they believe me? I was only a kid myself. The police would give Wills back to The Hand, because she was his mother. And guess who'd end up getting screwed?

Dee-deet.

I jumped. Wills kept on sleeping. I shifted him carefully and pulled out my phone.

"Hello?"

Nothing on the other end.

"Dad?"

"Where is it?" said a deep voice. Not Dad's.

"What?" I said. "Where is *what*? Who is this?"

"You know what I want," said the voice. "I want my money. And I want it *now*."

"Your—what? No, you—you have the wrong number."

And I hit the *off* button before I could hear that creepy voice again.

"What the hell was that?" I tossed my phone onto the bench like it was poison.

Then I gasped.

Money?

That fat stack of cash. The money that had disappeared by the time Jake caught up with The Hand. Could that creepy voice on the phone have been Jake's?

"That's impossible," I said out loud. "How would he get my phone number?"

And then another picture flashed in my mind.

My magazine.

The Hand had taken my magazine with her—the magazine I'd been scribbling on. Writing out my cell phone number so I wouldn't forget it.

Okay, so The Hand had my phone number, and now Jake had it too. But why did he think *I* had that money?

I looked down at my backpack.

With my free hand, I shifted it on the bench next to me and unzipped it. I dug around inside, identifying with my fingers the stuff I'd packed that morning: clean t-shirts, the rest of my magazines, water bottle . . . .

Then I felt it. Something papery, like a ragged notepad. But I hadn't packed a notepad. I pulled my hand out to see what I was holding.

"Holy crap."

A stack of bills.

The Hand's missing money. She hadn't flushed it away or lost it under the seats. She'd put it in *my* backpack. She must've done it while I was in the bathroom, just before the train stopped in Penn Station.

But why?

I riffled the corners of the bills. It was impossible to count so quickly, but it looked like all twenties.

A lot of them.

I stuffed it all deep into my pocket before anyone else saw it. Then I tried to think, but I wasn't very successful.

Dee-deet.

I held my breath and checked the caller ID.

It was Dad.

"Victoria?" he said. "Are you on the train?"

"What's going on there, Dad?"

"Everything's going to be okay. I told the police it was all a big mistake and that the baby is safe. I told them you're on the way back to New York right now. Officer Martinez will need to ask you some questions, that's all. Once you explain what happened, everything will be fine."

I couldn't say anything.

"Victoria? You *are* on the train now, aren't you?"

I took a deep breath.

"Not exactly."

"*What?* Now what?"

"Dad, listen to me! Wills' mother hurt him. She abandoned him. He's not safe with her."

"Why didn't you tell me that earlier?"

"I tried to!"

"Calm down, Victoria," he said. "Maybe he won't go back to his mother, anyway. His father's the one who reported the kidnapping."

His father? Did he mean Jake?

"Is he there, Dad? Wills' father? Have you seen him?"

"He's around here somewhere, I think. Officer Martinez asked both of us to wait here until you and the baby get back to New York. The poor guy is practically frantic about his little boy. No wonder, if the mother is abusive."

"Oh, God," I breathed. "Dad, please—"

"Honey, don't worry. I'm sure he'll drop the kidnapping charges once he hears exactly what happened. He seems like a reasonable person."

"Are you kidding me?" I squeaked. "You're going to trust a person like that?"

"Like what?" said Dad. "He's not well-off, certainly, but he looked okay."

How could he be so oblivious?

"Dad, you have to tell Officer Martinez that Wills is in danger."

"Victoria, how do you know that? We don't know these people. If you think the baby's not safe with his parents, I'm sure the police will take that into consideration."

"Wills doesn't need *consideration*. He needs someone to stand up for him."

"Victoria, that's not my concern. You're my daughter. *You're* my concern."

"Oh yeah? You weren't concerned about my six-hitter!"

"What?"

"Jake is lying. You tell the police, Dad. Tell them everything. *I'm* not flaking out on Wills."

"Victoria, for God's sake—here, why don't you explain it yourself? Officer Martinez is right here."

Theoretically it was a good idea, but my stomach just wasn't in it at the moment.

"Wait, Dad—"

There were shuffling and scraping noises on the other end.

"Hello, Miss Dowling? Vicki? This is Officer Martinez."

"Victoria."

"Right. Victoria. You're in the Newark train station, is that correct?"

I tried to breathe evenly. "Yes."

"Okay, listen to me. I want you to find the police kiosk in the main waiting room and wait there. Your dad and I will come to get you in my car. I'll radio Newark PD right now and let them know to expect you. Do you understand?"

What choice did I have? Besides, with Jake hanging around Penn Station, a police escort might not be such a bad idea.

"Okay," I said. "I understand." And I hung up.

Maybe I was jumping to conclusions. Maybe it wasn't Jake who reported the kidnapping. Maybe William's father was someone else. A decent person who really *was* worried about Wills and loved him and would take him away from

The Hand when he found out what kind of mother she really was.

"There's only one way to know for sure," I said out loud.

Careful not to wake him, I shifted Wills onto my shoulder, hiked up my backpack with its attached bag of diapers, and started walking.

The waiting room was noisy and crowded. There were businessmen with briefcases. College students with backpacks. Young women with babies and little kids of their own. One lady carried a boxed birthday cake. They were all absorbed in their own lives, and suddenly I would've been happy to trade places with any one of them.

I spotted the police kiosk at the far end and headed in that direction.

Dee-deet.

"Now what?"

I checked the caller ID, but it wasn't Dad. It said *Unknown Caller.*

My heart pounded. And even though most of me knew it was probably a terrible idea, one tiny part of me just had to know what he was going to say.

"Hello?" I croaked.

"I mean it," said the voice. "I want my money without any funny stuff, or the kid ends up in the river. Once he's returned to my loving care." And then I heard a low laugh.

That proved it. The voice was Jake's, and the money was Jake's, and Wills' father was Jake.

"I'm calling the police now and telling them everything," I said.

"You breathe a word to the police and he *will* go in the river," he said. "Besides, who'll believe you? You're a kidnapper. You're on TV and everything. Wait—there you are right now! You're standing in the door of the train...the brat's wiggling and crying, trying to get away ....You're scowling... you grab him tighter. You turn around and drag him inside the train ... the doors close ... the train leaves." He laughed at his own play-by-play. "You are *so* nailed."

Then the phone went dead.

And that big part of me that had known it'd be a terrible idea to answer the phone in the first place said, *You idiot, Victoria. Are you happy now?*

Was that really how it looked? Like Wills was struggling to get away, instead of me struggling not to drop him? That would support Jake's story, not mine.

I *was* nailed.

My phone buzzed.

"Oh good grief." I couldn't resist. I flipped it open.

New message.

I watched the screen while something downloaded. Finally, a video started playing.

It was shaky, and shot from a low angle, maybe waist high. I had trouble picking out details on the tiny screen, but I did see someone wearing a policeman's cap.

A voice—Jake's voice—was saying, "Please, officer. That's my baby out there somewhere. You need to find that girl before it's too late!"

"Calm down, sir," said the policeman. "I know you're upset. The kidnapper and the baby are both in Newark Police custody. They'll be back here soon."

"Thank God," said Jake. Then the camera focused on something else. Jake was holding Wills' teddy bear.

And then abruptly, the video ended.

I smacked the phone shut and rammed it into my back pocket.

"Jake's milking this for all it's worth," I muttered to myself. "He's making himself look innocent, and me look guilty. And the police are buying it!"

I wasn't walking toward a police *escort*. It was police *custody*. And they were eating out of Jake's hand.

Without really thinking, I veered away from the police kiosk and stepped behind a rack of schedules.

I searched the crowd but didn't see a policeman—yet.

I did see the birthday cake lady, sitting on a bench near the kiosk, chatting with a young woman who had a little boy about the same age as Wills.

I looked around for security cameras, but it didn't really matter. The police already had their evidence against me.

Then I noticed something on the schedule board, and an idea flashed in my brain.

I scanned the display of printed schedules on the rack, and pulled out the one I wanted. I shook it open with my free hand, carefully shifted Wills higher on my shoulder, and compared what I saw on the page with the schedule board.

I glanced back over to the bench. The girl and the kid and the birthday cake lady were still there.

I pulled out my cell phone and hit *redial*.

"Hello?"

"Hi, Dad, are you on your way?"

"Yes, honey. It'll take us another twenty minutes or so. Look for us right around three o'clock. Did you find a police officer?"

"I'm resting on the bench in the waiting room, right across from the police kiosk. Wills is pretty heavy."

I heard muffled voices for a few seconds, and then Dad again. "Stay there, honey. Officer Martinez will radio the Newark police, and they'll come to you."

I peeked over the rack again. "I'm wearing a denim miniskirt, sandals, and a red hoodie." Which was nothing like the jeans and T-shirt I was wearing now and in the surveillance video, but by the time they figured that out, it wouldn't matter. "And we're sitting next to an older lady with a bakery box on her lap."

"Got it," said Dad. "Thanks, honey. You're doing great." And I heard him repeating, "...miniskirt, red hooded sweatshirt. She has...oh, medium brown hair...average height...normal build..."

I snapped my phone shut. If there was one thing I could count on, it was Dad's dreadfully bad observation skills. He probably thought I still had braces.

I looked up, and sure enough, here came a cop out of the kiosk, toward the girl in the red hoodie.

Now I needed to move fast.

I walked up to the ticket window that was farthest from the police kiosk. I started to reach for my Bloomingdale's money, but stopped. Then I reached into my pocket and slid a bunch of twenties out of the middle of Jake's stack.

"Excuse me. How much is a ticket for the 2:43 train to Atlanta?"

NINE

Here's the way I figured it.

We were already in big trouble. In fact, things couldn't get much worse, unless—ironically—we did what everyone wanted us to do. But if we went back to New York now, we'd be walking into a trap.

I'd promised Wills I'd keep him safe. I knew what it felt like to be abandoned. Okay, I wasn't physically left behind the way Wills was, but what do you call it when your parents go off in two directions, leaving you dangling in the middle? When you have two beds and two toothbrushes and you never know where you left your favorite pair of jeans? Home can only be one place. And a home that's not safe is even worse than no home at all.

In a way, Wills and I were already homeless. So we left, and I made it official: I was a kidnapper.

I left my phone on. Dad would call again, and I wanted him to. If I was going to be a kidnapper, I needed to make my demands, even if it meant risking another call from Jake. I had to let people know this was serious.

The train started moving, and that's how easy it was to slip through their fingers.

I should've been scared to be alone with a little kid on a train heading to unknown territory. Well, I *was* scared. But I was even more scared of what would happen if we didn't run. This must have been the right thing to do, because I could finally breathe again. A little, anyway.

I unzipped my backpack and stared at Jake's cash. Then, with my hands inside my pack, I did a quick count.

"Whoa," I whispered to myself. "There's more than eight hundred dollars here."

Wills was waking up. I wrapped the rubber band around the money again and zipped my pack closed.

"Bye-bye?" he asked sleepily, blinking up at the window.

"Yes, buddy, we're going bye-bye. It's okay. I'm here for you."

He smiled at me. Then he sat up and started to kick the seat in front of him.

↔ ↔ ↔

Dad had said that he and Officer Martinez would get to the Newark station at about three o'clock.

At 3:02, my phone rang, right on cue.

"'Lo?" said William. Right on cue.

I took a deep breath and looked at him.

"No 'hello' right now, okay? I have to talk to my dad. Want another peanut butter cracker?"

Wills took the cracker, thank goodness. I hoped he'd stay busy with it long enough for me to get through this phone call. I hit the *talk* button.

But then I realized I hadn't looked at the caller ID, and maybe it was Jake on the other end and not Dad. I opened my mouth to talk, but nothing came out.

"Victoria?" said the voice.

I closed my eyes. "Hi, Dad."

"Honey, there's some sort of pile-up in the Lincoln Tunnel. It's total gridlock here. I don't know how long it'll take us to get there. Are you doing okay?"

I was suddenly feeling much better, actually.

"Yes, Dad." I tried to sound slightly disappointed. "The Newark police are very nice."

"Yeah, well, the Newark police told us that you're giving them a hard time. Arguing with them and insisting they have the wrong person. What's that all about?"

I cringed, and silently apologized to the girl in the red hoodie for screwing up her afternoon.

"Sorry, Dad. It's, uh, been a crazy day, you know? I got upset. I'm feeling better now, though."

"Okay, good. Just sit tight, and behave yourself. We'll be there as soon as we can."

I blew out my cheeks in relief. He'd bought it, for now.

Every minute I gained would get us another mile farther away.

But part of me wished it didn't have to be this way.

"Dad?"

"Yes, honey?"

"I had to do this, Dad. Wills isn't safe."

"Honey, you don't have to worry about that anymore. Officer Martinez promises the baby will be taken care of. He knows people in the Police Department, and in the Office of Family Services, and he's promised to make sure personally that the baby will be safe."

I almost said, "Oh great, Dad. You're a little late, though, because that train's already left the station, so to speak."

But what I really said was, "Can I talk to Officer Martinez?"

"That's a good idea, honey. Hang on."

There were muffled voices on the other end for a second.

"Victoria? This is Officer Martinez. Is everything all right? It's important that you cooperate with the officers in Newark until we get there."

I sighed. The girl in the hoodie was a mother. If she knew *why* she was being detained by the Newark cops, I bet she'd play along, for Wills' sake.

"Wills won't be safe if we come back to New York. His father is lying."

"Okay, Victoria. We'll take all that into consideration. If you want, you can testify in a hearing, and the judge will use your testimony to help decide the best place for the baby."

"What kind of place?"

"Maybe with another relative, if there is one. Maybe with a foster home. It'll be up to the judge to decide."

"What if the judge decides to give him back to his father?" I asked. "Can you promise me that won't happen?"

"I can make a recommendation, but it won't be my decision to make."

"Someone has to take responsibility for this little boy," I said.

"Lots of people will," said Officer Martinez.

"That doesn't sound like a good idea," I said, thinking out loud.

"I know what you're saying," said Officer Martinez. "Sometimes kids fall through the cracks. I'll do my best to make sure that doesn't happen."

I was learning all about falling through the cracks. Sometimes it works to your advantage. Sometimes not. "See, but that's not good enough," I said. "Wills is an innocent little boy. The world is a dangerous place."

"I know that, miss," said the officer. "I'll do whatever I can to help, but it's not all up to me."

"I get it," I said. "So that way, if he falls through the cracks, it won't be your fault."

"Miss Dowling," said Officer Martinez, "you need to trust that the system will do its job. You also need to realize that you don't have the right to keep that baby right now. No one will punish you if you took him by accident. But now you need to turn the matter over to us."

I shook my head. "Too many things can go wrong. I can't take that chance. I made a promise to Wills, and I won't break it."

"I respect that," said Officer Martinez. "But respect has to go two ways, don't you think? I'll admit I can't give you any guarantees. Life doesn't work that way. You just have to trust me."

"No guarantees?"

"I *will* guarantee to do my best."

I sighed. "I believe you."

"That's great. Why don't you tell your dad?"

There was a pause, and then I heard Dad's voice again.

"Honey? Officer Martinez told me the good news. You're ready to let him straighten everything out for you."

"No, Dad. I never said that."

"What? But he just—"

"Dad, he said he'd do his best, and I believe him. But what if that's not good enough? I'm not going to let Wills fall through the cracks. He's safe with me. I can take care of him."

"Victoria, you're being unreasonable. We'll talk about this when I get to Newark."

I closed my eyes. "I don't think so, Dad."

I waited for the explosion on the other end. But I only heard the sporadic blasts of car horns. When he spoke again, I could hear the anger growing in his voice.

"This needs to be done, Victoria."

"Why?"

"What do you mean, *why?* Because it's the right thing to do. It's the legal thing. I shouldn't have to tell you that. Let's end this now, Victoria, before it can't be undone."

"Sorry, Dad. It might be the legal thing, but it's not the *right* thing. I made a promise to Wills, and now we both need a promise from you, and the police, and all you grown-ups. Wills can't go back to his parents. He needs a safe, loving home for the rest of his life. Guarantee us those things, and I'll bring him back. Not until then."

"Young lady, you have no choice but to bring him back."

I bit my lip. The guy at the ticket window had made me show my school ID, and he'd typed my name onto my ticket. That meant I was probably in the Amtrak computer. And any minute now the police would figure out that the girl in the red hoodie really *was* the wrong person. But still, I was pretty sure that leaving on another train would be the last thing Dad would expect me to do.

"You're wrong, Dad. I do have a choice." I hit the *end* button and then the power button until the screen went dark. I dropped the phone into my lap.

"'Lo?"

William picked up the phone and held it to his peanut butter face. I folded myself in half and hung my head between my knees.

"I don't know, Wills. Was that a stupid thing to do? But Jake is waiting for us in New York, and Dad and the police are flaking out on us. We can do this. Everything is under control."

That last part might have been a lie. Until we got on this train, everything had been pretty much an accident. Now, things were different. I'd deliberately taken off with Wills when I knew it was against the law. It was only a matter of time before someone would think to check the Amtrak records.

Things were definitely getting more complicated.

Wills was rummaging through my backpack. He'd found the last peanut butter cracker and was crumbling it in his fist. Chunks of cracker and peanut butter dropped onto his lap. Cracker dust sprinkled the seat, my backpack, and the floor.

"Don't do that. You're making a mess."

"No."

"Come on, Wills. I don't feel like it right now. Be a good boy."

"No!" He threw what was left of the cracker onto the floor and he started to wail.

"What's wrong? Please don't cry ... tell me what you want ... "

I tried to hold him, but he kicked me and then he cried even louder. People stared at us. I could feel my face burning.

"Wills," I whispered. "Wills, please don't ... "

He kept up his tantrum. I couldn't get hold of him without getting kicked. I tried singing quietly to calm him down.

You are my sunshine …

"NO!"

He squirmed onto the floor at my feet and sprawled out on top of the cracker crumbs, where he just kept wailing.

And then I started to cry too.

Maybe things weren't quite so much under control after all.

TEN

It felt good to cry. I guess we needed it, because we both just let loose. I bent over in my seat and rubbed William's back, letting the tears drip off the tip of my nose onto the dirty floor. Wills finally quieted down to a soft sort of crying song. It was just too much tension for one day.

Finally, he stood up and rested his head on my knee. I brushed the crumbs and dirt out of his hair and off his overalls, and I lifted him onto my lap. He reached for my open backpack and pulled out a magazine.

"Book?" he said, and we settled in to do some reading.

The train kept rolling and the sun kept sinking. Every time we stopped, my heart pounded and I watched for police activity, but I never saw any. If we were lucky, Dad and Officer Martinez still thought we were somewhere in Newark.

I checked against the schedule—Trenton, Philly, Wilmington. Three more states gone, just like that. You'd think it would make me nervous, but the farther away we got from New York—and Jake—the calmer I felt.

When William got tired of the magazine, he stood up at the window and we played *I Spy*. Car. Birdie. Garbage truck—beeeeg garbage truck.

By Baltimore it was six o'clock and I was hungry.

"I'm starving." I picked him up. "Let's take a walk and get some supper."

There was a real diner car on this train, with tables and booths and hot food cooking. Roast chicken and potatoes and broccoli or some other stinky veggie. It smelled heavenly.

"Guess what? Dinner's on your mom and dad tonight."

"Mama?" he said.

I swallowed hard, trying to read his face. Did he miss her?

He didn't seem particularly sad. He didn't seem particularly happy. He just squished my cheeks between his hands, kissed my puckered lips, and said, "Eat?"

After dinner I left the waiter a ten-dollar tip.

We were settled back into our seats by the time the train stopped in D.C. Next came Alexandria, Virginia, and just like that, another state gone. For the first time in hours, I felt like I could almost breathe normally. We played some more *I Spy*. Airplane. Taxi. Fire truck—beeeeg fire truck.

I hadn't played that game since I was twelve years old.

◇ ◇ ◇

The summer I turned twelve, we took a family trip to the Grand Canyon. Dad called it a *once-in-a-lifetime experience*. I called it a *why can't I just stay home and hang at the pool with my friends experience*. Two hours to drive to LaGuardia, five hours on the plane to Phoenix, four hours driving through the desert in 112-degree heat. I was pretty sure we were going to way too much trouble to see a big ol' hole in the ground in the middle of God-forsaken nowhere.

But Dad wouldn't give up. During breakfast one morning, he disappeared and came back a few minutes later wearing the biggest, whitest cowboy hat ever manufactured. Just as I was thinking I couldn't possibly be more mortified, he whipped an identical hat out of a shopping bag and stuck it on my head, right there in the coffee shop, which was thankfully about a zillion miles from anyone who knew me. Mom laughed and said she couldn't wait to wear her new beaded moccasins. He was so pleased with himself.

An hour later, we were on a tram with thirty other sweaty tourists, staring at—*ta DA!*—a big ol' hole in the ground. I tried to be impressed, but it just wasn't working. Well, it *was* impressive, but in a huge, impossible-to-grasp sort of way. The canyon seemed to go on forever and ever and ever, so that you had no perspective. It looked two-dimensional and fake. I felt like I was in an IMAX theater where the air conditioning was broken. I couldn't get my eyes or my brain around it.

We stayed on the tram for a while. Dad and I bumped the brims of our hats together whenever we turned our heads. Mom's camera clicked every time we went around a bend, and I was pretty sure that when we got home, the pictures would all look exactly the same.

That's when Dad fired up a game of *I Spy*. It'd been one of my favorites when I was little, and he knew it. Now he was riffling through his guidebook, then he was pointing, saying, "Who can find...a peregrine falcon!...a mule deer!...Anyone who sees a Gila monster gets double ice cream!" Suddenly I was grateful to have a giant hat to hide under. But then I sort of got into it, and by the end of the day Dad owed me a triple ice cream for spotting a rattlesnake sleeping under a scrubby bush.

I held Dad to his promise, and that evening we all stood at a railing, eating ice cream and watching the sinking sun throw long shadows into the canyon. The temperature was dropping too, and I shivered from the cool air on my skin and the ice cream in my stomach.

But I was happy. I was happy to have my gigantic goofy cowboy hat just like Dad's, and happy to be followed around by Mom with her sunscreen and her napkins and her camera. We were still a family then. Did I mention I was happy?

And then something amazing happened. As the sun sank lower, its motion seemed to speed up, so that by the time it reached the horizon, you could actually see it moving, this giant orange ball teetering on the edge of the canyon. Suddenly the huge, fake-looking, two-dimensional hole in the ground became three-dimensional—seared with bright light and dark shadow, so that every rock and ledge and crag stood out in blinding relief. I gasped, because suddenly the Grand Canyon was … well, it was so incredibly … grand.

"Oh, Daddy," I breathed, and I threw my arms around his neck, knocking both our hats to the ground. He laughed and hugged me tight.

"Was it worth the trip?" he said.

I nodded. Because it really was.

And suddenly I couldn't stop hugging him. More than I'd ever wanted anything in my whole life, I wanted this one moment to last forever.

"Everything is so perfect. Please don't ever let go, Daddy."

He held me close, and his whiskers brushed my cheek.

"Never, baby girl," he whispered. "Never in a million years."

"Look!" said Mom.

We turned in time to see the last sliver of sun disappear below the horizon. In the space of a few seconds, the blazing light was gone and the desert all around us went black and that vast awesome canyon just totally vanished.

"Whoa!" said one of the other tourists left in the dark. "Where'd it go?"

I felt around for Dad, who was bent over trying to

find our cowboy hats. He stood up, and as my eyes adjusted to the faint light from the lodge behind us, I could see him smiling. He put my hat on Mom's head. Then he took my hand, and Mom took my other hand, and we walked toward the light of the lodge and supper.

We were still a family, and I was happy.

That was the last time I played *I Spy*, until today, with Wills.

↔ ↔ ↔

By Manassas, it was dark outside and Wills was getting sleepy. I pulled a sweatshirt out of my pack and spread it out on the seat for him. Then I rolled up one of my t-shirts and tied the sleeves together to make a pillow. He settled in, and I sang to him softly until he fell asleep.

You are my sunshine
My only sunshine…

Culpeper, Charlottesville, Lynchburg. I turned off the reading lamp and closed my magazine. I stuffed it into my pack, and that's when I saw my cell phone. I hadn't thought about it for hours. Somehow I'd managed to forget all about Jake, and Dad, and the police.

Now I turned the phone over in my hand and was so tempted to turn it on and call Dad, just to let him know that Wills and I were okay.

But it was so nice not to feel nervous or scared, even if it would only last a little while. If I turned it on now to call Dad, everything would just start up again. Or Jake might call again. Besides, it was late. One thing I knew for sure: we'd be in the same situation in the morning.

I left the phone in my backpack and put it all on the floor. Then I curled up alongside Wills and closed my eyes.

 ELEVEN

When I woke up, the sky was gray and my neck was stiff. Wills was still sleeping, sprawled across both seats. It was a wonder one of us hadn't fallen onto the floor.

Outside, there were hills covered with tall pine trees on both sides of the train. Every once in a while we passed a clearing with a small house or a farmer's field. The plowed dirt was a rusty bright orange color. The moist smell of pine forest pushed its way inside the train car.

"Whoa," I whispered to myself. "We really did it. We're way far away."

It was 6:45 AM. I checked the schedule: Spartanburg next, then Greenville, then Clemson. In a little over two hours we'd be in Atlanta, and then we'd either have to get off the train or buy a new ticket. I had no problem spending Jake's money, but I didn't want to go too far if we didn't have to. Maybe Dad and Officer Martinez would find a way to meet my demands. Shouldn't I at least give them the chance to tell me about it, before we ended up in Miami or South America or someplace? I decided I'd wait another hour or so and then call, to see if they were making any progress.

Wills stretched, and then he opened his eyes and looked around.

"Tee?" he said, sitting up and looking a little bit scared. Then he saw me, and he relaxed.

"Hi," he said.

There was that name again. Who was Tee, anyway? I didn't think it was The Hand—he called her Mama. Maybe Tee was a little friend or something.

"Good morning." I couldn't help smiling at his sleepy face. "Did you have a good night's sleep?"

"Seep." He nodded, standing up on the seat and pushing his face against the window. Then he tilted his head up and pressed his cheek against the glass, trying to see the tops of the trees as we went by.

"Beeeeg," he said.

"Yeah, you're right about that. Big trees."

"Beeeeg trees!"

"Oh, you are just so smart!" I snuffled my nose into his neck until he squealed.

"Are you hungry? Let's go get some breakfast."

The dining car wasn't open yet, so we went to the café

car and got some little boxes of cereal, milk, and a banana. Wills squished his half of the banana before he ate it.

He was looking a little ragged again. There was milk on his chin and banana between his fingers. His overalls were gray from his temper tantrum under the seat the day before, and his hair was almost too sticky to brush. I'd been keeping him in clean diapers, but even the baby powder wasn't doing a very good job with the smell any more. I wasn't smelling too fresh myself.

The train was slowing down. According to the schedule, the next stop was Gainesville, Georgia, and already I could see the outskirts of a town in the valley below us. The streets were laid out neatly, with houses and sidewalks and gas stations. I could see the town center, where there was a little park, with grass and benches and a clock tower. After Gainesville, the next stop would be Atlanta, and I'd have to make some more decisions.

Soon after we passed the town center, the train slowed even more, and then we were in the Gainesville station. The train slid past someone wearing a tan shirt and dark brown pants, with glints of shiny things near the shoulder and on the belt.

A uniform. Some kind of policeman or patrolman or security guard.

The train squealed to a stop.

My brain instantly went into high gear. We were maybe six cars ahead of the policeman. Was he looking for us?

Instinctively, I looked up. I'd forgotten all about security cameras. Were there cameras on the train? Maybe they'd been watching us all along, and knew exactly where we were. Maybe Jake knew too.

My mouth went dry.

Then another nagging thought made me pull out my train ticket and stare at my name typed on it. By now, it must have occurred to Officer Martinez to search the Amtrak records for my name.

"You idiot, Victoria," I hissed under my breath. Of course the police were looking for us. They were probably checking stops all along the line.

I grabbed my backpack.

"Come on, Wills. Wanna go for a walk?"

"Walk!" he yelled, jumping on the seat. I scooped him up, stepped to the door, and peeked out. As soon as I saw the man in brown step onto the car at the back end of the train, we jumped off.

I dashed for the ladies' room just across the platform, and we hid in a stall until I could hear the train pulling away.

"Down," said Wills.

"Shhh! Can you play a quiet game?" I whispered. "Like this?" And I clamped my hand over my mouth. Wills giggled and did it too.

We sat in the stall with our hands over our mouths, listening to men's voices out on the platform. I couldn't understand what they were saying, but they were getting closer. I leaned back on the seat and pulled my feet up. I prayed I could hold my balance and not fall in, backpack, baby, and all. I gave Wills a serious look, and he kept quiet.

The bathroom door squeaked open, but I didn't hear any footsteps. After a few seconds the door squeaked again and the voices faded away.

I tiptoed toward the bathroom door and opened it a crack, but I didn't see the policeman. He must have gone into the station. I opened the door wider. Still nobody. I noticed a rack of schedules on the wall, so I grabbed one of each. Then, with Wills bouncing on my arm, I hustled around the corner of the building and started walking in the general direction of the town center.

After half a block we came to an intersection. The sign said Main Street. I checked over my shoulder, but didn't see anyone. I turned up Main Street and ran, with Wills bouncing in my arms, until we were past the first house and the train station was out of sight.

"Down," said Wills again, kicking.

I set him down on the sidewalk, and he took off like he'd been let out of a cage. I sort of knew how he felt.

It was a pretty street—wide and straight, with a sidewalk on one side and lined with big leafy trees and neat, small houses. I figured since it was called Main Street it might lead downtown eventually, so I decided to keep going.

I jogged after Wills. "Stay on the sidewalk!"

He laughed and kept running. Every few seconds he would glance around to see if I was still chasing him, then he'd squeal and run a little faster. Before I knew it, I was laughing too. We'd managed to ditch the police, at least for a little while.

Just before we got to the next corner, I grabbed him

around the ribs and swung him in a big circle. He squealed and laughed some more, and once we were across the street I set him down and he started running again. It felt so good to run, and to laugh, and to worry about nothing except me and Wills.

After a couple of blocks we slowed down to a walk. The morning air was cool and heavy, as if someone had dropped a damp washcloth over the world. I inhaled deeply and smelled earth and dusty pine needles.

On the last block, Main Street widened and the yards got bigger. The houses were bigger too—white with black shutters and dark green doors. Some of the houses even had round columns in front, just like in old movies. The lawns were bright green and edged with flowers—pink and white and blazing red. Even some of the trees were blooming, with papery clusters of hot pink flowers.

The sun was getting higher and already it was warm. I pulled the thick moist air deep into my lungs. Two kids zipped past on their bikes, and then popped wheelies in the middle of the street. Somehow, watching them do normal kid stuff helped me relax a little, too.

Then I saw a car turn the corner and drive slowly toward us.

A patrol car.

There was no place to go. I took William's hand and bent down, pretending to wipe his nose, trying my best to hide both our faces. I heard the engine get louder, and then hum steadily. The car had stopped. I couldn't breathe.

"Hey, you two," called a stern voice.

I straightened up, but still couldn't bear to turn around. How did I ever think we'd be able to hide?

"Go home and get your bike helmets," called the voice again. "Y'all know that's the law. And watch out for cars, or I'll be calling your folks next."

I heard the squeal of bike tires, and then I heard the car's engine rev a little and fade away. I peeked through my hair and watched the patrol car continue down the street and turn the next corner. The two kids watched from their bikes, too. Then they did a U-turn and kept popping wheelies. I swallowed my heart and lungs back into place.

"Holy crap. Are we ever going to be able to relax? I wish we could just blend in and stay here forever."

But as soon as the words came out of my mouth, I knew it would never happen. I hadn't admitted it, even to myself, but I'd known all along that sooner or later we'd have to go back. Back to the real world, where everyone was waiting for us. Where Wills and I didn't belong together.

Still, I wished it. I wished we could stay forever in Gainesville, Georgia, where nobody cared what kind of trouble we were in back home. Where it was quiet and peaceful and green. Where Wills and I could trust each other and count on each other. Where I'd never bruise him or be mean to him. I'd never break a promise to him, and he'd love me for it because he'd know that it meant I loved him too. And I'd never, ever move away to the big city so that he'd only be able to visit me on long weekends and over summer vacation, or make him choose between one home or another. Wills and I would be a real family, and this would be our home, and we'd be safe and happy. I wished it as hard as I'd ever wished for anything. And all the while I knew it would never come true.

Wills finally ran out of gas. He plopped down right in someone's front yard, all spread-eagle on the shady grass. He looked so happy.

"Come on, my handsome prince." I stood him up and held his hand and pointed to what I saw at the end of the block—the town green and the clock tower.

Just then, the clock chimed eight times and brought me back to reality.

I sighed. I really needed to make a phone call. But I pushed the thought out of my head.

"Just a little while longer," I said out loud.

Was it so bad to want one peaceful morning?

 TWELVE

The Gainesville, Georgia town square was—a giant square. One whole city block was all grass and flower beds, with two criss-crossing brick paths that cut a big X right through the center. The clock tower stood in the middle of the X. People hurried across the square, wearing suits and carrying steaming cups of coffee, even though it was already getting hot. There was a big stone building on one side of the square, with the words HALL COUNTY COURT HOUSE carved across the top.

I decided we'd walk in the opposite direction of the court house.

We toured around the square—bank, laundromat, ice cream shop, antique store, drugstore, coffee shop, jewelry store, law office, law office, law office, and back to the courthouse. It was only 8:15, so they were all closed, except the coffee shop. And the courthouse. Which reminded me of what I had to do this morning.

"Come on, Wills," I sighed. "Time to make a phone call."

We crossed back over to the park and found a bench that was off by itself. I sat down and plopped my backpack onto my lap, while Wills sat in the grass and picked clover.

I opened my pack.

There was my phone, under the slowly shrinking package of diapers. I stared at it for a long time before I finally pulled it out.

"I don't want to do this," I sighed.

Wills was smelling a clover flower. Practically the whole thing was stuck up his nose. Then he sneezed.

"Bless you," I said, and my voice was already shaky. But I had to call Dad, to tell him we were okay. And to see if he'd come up with any ideas. I took a deep breath and turned the phone on.

The little screen glowed with the words *23 missed calls.*

"Good grief," I said. "Didn't anyone get any sleep last night?"

There was also a picture message.

I couldn't resist. I hit the *view message* button and waited for the download.

At first it was hard to see on the tiny screen, but then I

knew what it was. It was Wills' teddy bear—the one that had been in The Hand's canvas bag. Its head had been torn off.

"Very subtle, Jake," I muttered.

I didn't want to know how many of those other twenty-three calls were from Jake. Not bothering to check the voice mails, I hit the *contacts* button to find Dad's number.

Dee-deet.

"'Lo?" Wills said, looking up. He had pollen on his nose.

I gulped.

Dee-deet.

"'Lo!" said William, standing up and pushing the phone to my face. I frowned at him and checked the caller ID.

I took a deep breath and hit the *talk* button.

"Dad?"

"Victoria! Where have you been? We've been up all night trying to reach you!"

I almost said "No kidding," but what I really said was, "Why? Have you come up with a way to meet my demands?" Because I was still really mad at him, but I was also hoping he'd figured a way out of this mess.

"Victoria, listen. The police have talked to Danny's mother."

"Who?" But I knew exactly who.

"Danny's mother. The baby's mother. What made you think his name was William, anyway?"

I closed my eyes and shook my head. "Where is she?"

"Somewhere here in New York City. The baby's father helped the police find her. Honey—Victoria, you need to know that her story doesn't agree with yours. She says she never abandoned the baby—that she turned around to get her things, and when she turned back, he was gone."

"What? Dad, she's lying! Don't you believe me?"

"I honestly don't know what to believe. Right now it's her word against yours."

"My word should count for more than hers," I said, "At least to you."

"Of course it does, Victoria. But the police need more than that. They need evidence. And you have to look at it this way—who's cooperating with the police here, and who isn't?"

I hated him for saying that. Especially because he was right.

Then I remembered something. "What about the surveillance video? Wouldn't that be evidence?"

"That's the other thing," said Dad. "Officer Martinez showed me the video. It shows you in the doorway of the train, struggling with the baby, and then the train leaves. It looks—" He sighed. "It looks like you—snatched the baby."

So Jake's description had been right.

"But Dad—"

I heard a giggle. Wills handed me a clover flower. Then he hugged my knee and smiled.

"Sorry, kid," I said to him. "That's not evidence. It's just your opinion."

"What?" said Dad.

"Isn't there video of Jake? Or The Hand? Are there cameras inside the trains?"

"Officer Martinez said the cameras are only on the platforms," said Dad. "And it all depends on where people are standing, which way the camera's pointing....There's nothing else so far." He sounded defeated.

"This is crazy, Dad!" I said. "That video doesn't tell the whole story!"

Dad sighed loudly, and then he was quiet for a long time. Suddenly I felt so bad about everything I was putting him through. But what about Wills? How could it be wrong to stand up for a two-year-old who couldn't stand up for himself?

"Victoria, listen," Dad finally said in a quiet voice. "You know I'll fight for you no matter what. But you have to understand. The evidence doesn't look good. We need you here to tell your side of the story."

Now my own voice was quiet. "How can I do that? I promised Wills I'd protect him. He'll be in danger if I bring him back. Please, Dad."

"His name is Danny, and he's *not* your responsibility. You've had only the slightest glimpse into his family and his life, and suddenly you think you know what's best for him? You're meddling in strangers' lives, and you're messing up your own life in the process. Is that worth it, Victoria?"

"Yes!" I said. "Because he's helpless, and the world is a dangerous place, and I know what he needs."

"What makes you think *you* know what he needs?" Dad said.

"Because *I* need—"

I don't know why I stopped myself. Maybe I was surprised to have to tell my own father that Wills and I needed exactly the same things. Love. Security. One place to call home. Someone to help us feel safe in an unsafe world.

Or maybe I was just too stubborn to admit it. So I stopped myself, and instead I said, "Because *all* kids need to be safe, Dad."

"You know what's not safe?" he said. "Two kids running around all over the place by themselves, *that's* not safe."

Somehow he'd managed to miss the point completely.

"I *tried* to find you at the very beginning. You weren't there, remember? Or should we look for that on the video?"

"Young lady—" and then he stopped. "Okay, you're right," he finally said, more calmly. "It was my job to meet you at Penn Station, and if I'd done that, none of this would've happened."

"It did happen, though," I said, blinking hard. "Wills needs me, Dad, and I'm not going to flake out on him. I won't let him fall through the cracks."

"That job is too big for one fifteen-year-old girl. Lots of people here want to help you. Let's work on this together."

"Dad, I—" and the phone beeped in my ear.

Another call.

I checked the screen. *Unknown Caller*, but I knew exactly who it was.

"Victoria?" I heard Dad's voice. "Did you hear me?"

And if I needed any reminders of why Wills and I were a thousand miles from home and couldn't go back, I just got one.

Jake.

"Dad, you still don't get it. Jake is going to hurt Wills. I told you what has to happen before we come home. I haven't gotten this far just to turn around and—"

"What do you mean? How far *have* you gotten?"

I bit my bottom lip hard, and then I hit the *end* button on the phone.

"Crap! Now he knows for sure that we're not just hanging out in Newark or someplace nearby. If they haven't checked with Amtrak so far, they will now. Why did I do that?"

Because I was so upset about all the things that Dad said. About Jake and his threats over a stupid eight hundred bucks. About The Hand and the way she'd lied to the police.

"She did lie, right?" I said out loud.

"Right," said Wills. Now he was playing with the zippers of my backpack.

"At least someone's on my side," I said to him. "The world is flat, right?"

"Right!"

"That's what I thought."

I tried to remember exactly what had taken place in

Penn Station. It was already jumbled in my memory. But when I closed my eyes I could still see her, standing on the platform, alone. And I could see Wills in the bathroom, alone.

What are you supposed to do when you see a baby alone in a stinky toilet on a train? Leave him there?

Maybe.

I guess I could've yelled for the conductor or a security guard, or pulled the emergency alarm, or something.

But then The Hand had come back to the train, right before it pulled out of the station.

Jake had come back too, looking for the money. But maybe The Hand was looking for Wills. Maybe she did leave the money on the train, figuring Jake would haul her back to look for it, and then she could get her kid. And I screwed that up for her.

Because I took him.

"Oh, God. Is that what she's saying? That she was just hiding you from Jake? But I took you away. I *am* a kidnapper."

"Eat?" said Wills, practically stuffing his whole head inside my backpack. I looked at his tender bruised arms.

"I think we're out of snacks, buddy. Okay, so maybe The Hand *was* telling the truth. Sort of. But she also left a two-year-old alone on the train. What about that? And who knows what Jake would have done if he'd found you?" I pulled Wills out of my backpack and looked into his bottomless eyes. "If it happened again, I'd do it all over again. There's no way I could have just left you there."

"Down."

Wills bent down and picked up a green caterpillar. He held it about an inch from his face, inspecting it, and then he held it up for me to see. Without really thinking, I flipped my phone open, centered Wills on the screen, and snapped a photo. Then I zoomed in and snapped a close-up of his bruised arm. I hit *save* and then I shut the phone off.

"Bug?" said Wills.

"What? Yeah, that's a caterpillar bug."

"Bug," he said again, satisfied. Then he opened his mouth.

"Wills!"

He looked up at me.

"Wills? Don't eat the bug, honey." I gently took the caterpillar and set it down on the grass. "Do you want something to eat?"

"Eat!" he said, hopping up and down.

I looked down at stinky, bug-eating, beautiful Wills, and my heart did its own little hop. I was doing the right thing. They might be able to trace our train ticket, but we were already out of their reach. And out of Jake's reach. Suddenly, I was starving too.

"Come on. Let's go eat." I took his hand and we walked across the square toward the coffee shop.

Me and Wills.

THIRTEEN

We split a ham and cheese omelet, fruit salad, chocolate milk, sausage links, hot biscuits, orange juice, and grits. William's favorite was the grits. Not for eating. For squishing. After I tasted them, I could see why.

By the time we finished, Wills was a complete mess. There was egg in his ear, bits of biscuit down his overalls, and grits everywhere. I couldn't help giggling at him.

"Hey," I said. "I know what we can do. Come on."

We stepped out into the hot sunshine. I scanned the stores around the square, until I spotted what I was looking for.

I took William's hand and we walked across the square.

The laundromat was bright and clean and smelled like

fabric softener. It had a change machine, and a vending machine with packets of detergent and bleach and other laundry stuff. A line of plastic chairs stood by the front windows, and there was a bathroom in the back. Thank goodness. I could change clothes and wash the ones I was wearing. And in the bathroom, I discovered something even better.

"A sink!"

It was one of those big, deep wash basins like the one my grandma had in her basement. I turned on the faucet and waited. Sure enough, warm water.

"Oh, Wills…" I sang. "Guess what?"

"What?" he said, pushing the buttons on the vending machine just outside the bathroom door.

"How'd you like a bath?"

"Bath?" he said, poking his finger into the change return slot.

"Wouldn't that feel so good?" I said to him. "I wish I could join you, but we'd better not take public nakedness too far. Hey—what could we wash you with?"

The vending machine only had laundry supplies. It probably wasn't a good idea to give him a bath in laundry detergent, and end up stinging his eyes or giving him a rash or something.

"And yet," I said, bending down and rubbing noses with him, "it's probably just the industrial-strength cleaner we need to clean up your stink."

"Stink!" said Wills, hopping again.

"I wonder if the drugstore is open yet."

We took another walk. In the drugstore, we headed for the aisle with the travel sizes.

"Ha! Baby shampoo," I said. "We could wash your whole little bod with this. And look: 'no more tears'!"

"No no no tears!" said William, doing his hopping thing again. For a second I almost believed he knew what he was talking about.

"Let's go!" I cheered.

"Let go go!" he cheered back.

"Hold on now, Handful-and-a-Half. What else do we need while we're here? What about a washcloth? And a towel? Did you ever think of that, your highness?"

"Go go go!"

"You exhaust me."

"What?"

"Never mind. Come on."

We cruised the aisles and I considered the possibilities. Paper towels ... more baby wipes ... toilet paper?

"Ball?" he said as we passed the toy aisle.

"You want a ball?" I asked him. "Okay. Every kid needs a toy, right?" I tossed a little plastic football into our basket.

"Book?" said Wills.

"How can I turn that down?" I let him choose two little cardboard books.

"Truck?"

"Sure, why not? It's all on You-Know-Who."

In the next aisle, something caught my eye and I screeched to a halt.

"What do you think?" I asked Wills, pointing to a display. "Yes or no?"

"No," he said.

I considered.

"I think yes." I selected a pair of scissors and put them into our shopping basket.

And then I spotted the perfect thing for his bath.

"Automotive cleaning rags!" I declared. "Listen to this: *Untreated soft cotton. Twelve inch squares. Ideal for washing, waxing, and polishing. Package of five. Only $2.49.*"

I waved the bundle in front of Wills. "Ha! We can use one to wash you and the rest to dry you. And then we can use them for other stuff later. Are we geniuses or what?"

"What!"

"Right!"

It was still early, and the laundromat wasn't very busy, thank goodness. We went into the bathroom and locked the door. Then I sat Wills on the floor and gave him a magazine to read while I got busy.

I pulled the rubber band off Jake's shrinking stack of cash and used it to tie my hair into a loose ponytail. Then I found the scissors, reached behind me, and went to work. It took two strokes.

"Just like Mary Queen of Scots," I said out loud. Which made me realize I'd learned something in European History after all.

I chucked the dismembered ponytail into the trash barrel and got ready to change my clothes.

"No peeking, now," I said to Wills.

"No," he said, turning the pages of the magazine.

But I couldn't stand the thought of putting clean clothes on my grubby body. I tore open the package of rags, turned on the water, and washed up at the sink with some of the baby shampoo. I even washed my hair. Wills sat quietly reading his horoscope.

As I worked the warm suds through my chopped hair, my mind relaxed and wandered.

↔ ↔ ↔

Dad was canned right after our Grand Canyon trip. Our trip of a lifetime. All the big insurance companies in Hartford were cutting back.

That fall, when school started, I didn't dare ask for any new clothes. I didn't even make a Christmas list. I just wore the same jeans and T-shirts over and over and I prayed that no one at school would notice, which any sixth grade girl in the entire world knows is utterly hopeless. Mom said, "Victoria, what does it matter as long as you're clean? With shiny clean hair and a fresh glowing face, no one will care what you're wearing."

Nice try.

I did my best to ignore what people said behind my back at school. Courteney Black almost became Courteney Black Eye when she asked me out loud in the lunch line if I went with my mom to pick up the welfare checks. The cafeteria monitor stepped in just in time, and said, "Victoria, what on earth has gotten into you? I've known you since kindergarten, and you've always been the sweetest girl. But if you start a fight I'll have to have you suspended."

It would've been worth it.

That January, Dad took a job with a company in New York City, and started commuting from Connecticut. It could've been worse, I guess. He almost got a job in Chicago.

Dad commuted to New York every day for almost two years. Now he lives there, and Mom and I still live in Connecticut, and I have plenty of money to buy plenty of clothes. But somehow I still end up wearing mostly jeans and T-shirts. Maybe I'm just waiting for Courteney Black Eye to try opening her mouth one more time.

I pulled my clean clothes out of my pack and got dressed. Then I gathered everything up and we stepped out of the laundromat bathroom. I got five dollars' worth of quarters from the change machine and bought little packages of laundry detergent and fabric softener. Then I stripped Wills down to his diaper and threw all our clothes into a washing machine with the detergent. Wills put the quarters in the slots and pushed the buttons.

"Okay, my handsome prince," I whispered to him as we headed back to the bathroom. "Your turn for a bath!"

An hour later Wills and I were back outside. The sun was high and the air was steamy hot. Our clothes were clean, our bodies were clean, our hair was clean, and we both smelled like baby shampoo and fabric softener. It was heavenly.

"So this is what you really look like." I hugged him.

"No," he whined, shaking his head. "Down."

"What's the matter? Do you need a nap? We did get up pretty early this morning."

We headed back to the square and found a secluded spot under a tree. I spread my freshly washed T-shirt on the grass and sat William down on it, then I lay down on the grass next to him. The breeze was warm, but my damp hair kept me cool, especially in the shade. William's hair was almost dry already, but he didn't seem to mind the heat. It only took about a minute for him to lie down too. He blinked his heavy eyelids.

"Shine?" he said to me.

"What?" I asked, stroking his hair. It was all fluffy, and dark golden where patches of sunlight touched it.

"Shine," he said again. "Sunshine?"

"Oh! You are my sunshine?"

"Shine," he said, smiling and closing his eyes.

I stroked his head and sang the song. He sang along on the last word of every line, so his song sounded like this:

Sunshine sunshine
Happy gray
Know dear, love you
Sunshine away.

And then he was asleep.

I sat up and leaned against the tree, watching his back rise and fall. It had been a good morning, considering. I'd fed him, and bathed him, and sang him to sleep on the shady grass.

His name was Danny. But he let me call him Wills.

FOURTEEN

The heat was getting to me. I could barely resist the urge to stretch out on the cool grass next to Wills and go to sleep, but I knew that wasn't a good idea. I was responsible for Wills and I had to keep an eye on him. Besides, if you want to avoid being arrested for kidnapping, it's probably not a good idea to get yourself hauled in for vagrancy because you took a nap in front of a courthouse.

Maybe some juicy gossip would keep me awake. I pulled one of my mags out of my backpack and leaned back against the tree to read.

And then I thought about my phone.

Who'd made the twenty-three calls? Was it all Dad?

Maybe if he left messages, I'd get some clues about what was going on in New York.

I turned the phone on and scrolled through the menus. The list of missed calls came up, and I quickly scanned the numbers.

A bunch of messages from Dad. A bunch more from Mom. Dad must have told her everything, and she was probably going crazy with worry, but that was her usual mode anyway, and I didn't have time to think about that right now.

Two calls were from the 212 area code, which was Manhattan. Probably Officer Martinez or some NYPD number. A text message from Unknown Caller: *Your screwd he goin in the River.*

"I love you too, Jake." I kept scrolling through the messages.

There was one number I didn't recognize at all. It was a 347 area code, which I didn't know. I knew for sure that it wasn't Connecticut, and it wasn't Manhattan.

I highlighted the 347 number for more information. The person had called at 4:22 AM. And left a message. I hit the voice mail button and waited.

"Hey. It's me," a voice said. A female voice. "Sorry about the trouble. And the money. But I had to do something quick, and I could tell Danny liked you. Call this number. She'll know what to do."

And she gave a phone number with another area code I didn't recognize. Then I heard the voice mail computer say, "End of message."

I stared at the phone like I'd just gotten a call from space aliens. Which, frankly, would have been less surprising than getting a call from The Hand, because that's whose voice it was.

I replayed the message. Then I dug out a pen and listened a third time. I smoothed out my magazine and wrote down the phone number that The Hand had told me to call.

Then I turned the phone off and dropped it onto the grass. I stared at the magazine, and the phone number written on it. The pages fluttered in the warm breeze.

"What's *that* all about?"

For reasons she hadn't bothered to share with me, the Hand had dumped eight hundred dollars of probably stolen money on me and then she'd given my phone number to Jake. What did she want now? I couldn't imagine a single reason why she'd give me a phone number, except to get me into more trouble.

Besides, even if I wanted to call the number, I'd have to turn on my phone again, and I didn't feel like hearing it ring. I didn't want to talk to Dad *or* to Jake.

"Oh, good grief." I leaned over and pulled the magazine toward me. I stared at the number scribbled on the cover.

Maybe if I dialed it really fast....

"Are you crazy?" I whispered again. "She's setting you up."

For what? What more trouble could she possibly get me into?

I leaned over and checked Wills. He was asleep on the grass, snoring softly. I picked up my phone.

"Okay, here goes." I hit the *on* button and dialed.

"Hello?"

It was a woman's voice. But it wasn't The Hand.

I swallowed hard. "Hello? Uh, you don't know me, but someone gave me this phone number ... "

"Someone gave you *my* phone number? I'm sorry, but I do all my charitable giving through my church."

"No, wait. That's not it." How was I going to explain this without sounding like a complete nut case? "I ... I don't know her name, but she has a little boy who's about two years old, I guess, with big brown eyes and fat cheeks?"

"Is this about Danny?"

Bingo.

"Yes, it's Danny."

"Has something happened to my grandnephew?"

"No, he's fine."

"Who did you say you are?" the voice asked. "Are you from Family Services?"

"What? No." I shook my head. "Wi—Danny's mother gave me this phone number when she—"

"Sandra Jean? Why isn't she calling me about her own child?"

"I don't know. I don't even know her. I just found the baby."

"You just 'found' the baby? Where did you find him?" She didn't sound upset, really. Just sort of exasperated.

"On a train. In Penn Station. In New York. She...kind of left him on the train."

"That doesn't sound like something a person can 'kind of' do. Talk plain to me, young lady."

I almost said "Yes, ma'am," even though I'd never said that to anyone in my life. She had the kind of voice that made you sit up straight.

"Okay—well—she just left him on the train. She stuck him in the bathroom and then she got off the train and walked away. It wasn't an accident, or a mistake. She did it on purpose." That was as plain as I could make it. Or my version of it, anyway.

"And how do you know all this?"

"I saw it. I watched them almost the whole time on the train. I couldn't help it."

"I see. So you found Danny. Where is he now?"

"He's here, with me. He's fine. I'm taking care of him."

"How old are you?"

I cleared my throat. "Fifteen."

"And where are you now? Penn Station, did you say?"

I almost hung up the phone. But there was something about her voice that stopped me. It was calm and teacher-ish and—so far—she sounded totally unsurprised by anything I said. So I shut my eyes and said, "We're in Georgia."

There was a silence at the other end for a second or two. Then she said, "Young lady, I think you'd better start at the beginning."

She was the first person in two days who didn't yell at me and jump to all sorts of conclusions before I could get six words out of my mouth. So I told her. It all came spilling out—beginning in Hartford and ending in Georgia and every place in between. I told her about William's bruises. I told her about Jake the Wall, and how I was afraid he'd hurt Wills. I told her about The Hand—Sandra Jean—hiding Jake's eight hundred dollars in my backpack without my knowing it. I told her about our accidental ride to Newark and our on-purpose ride to Georgia. I told her about the demands I made as an accused kidnapper. I told her about Jake's threatening phone calls. But not in detail. I didn't want to scare her, and I especially didn't want to sound like I couldn't handle things.

When I finally stopped, there was a long silence.

"Hello?" I said.

"Oh, I'm here. Just trying to soak it up, that's all."

"I know. I'm really sorry. It's gotten so complicated. I was just trying to protect William. Do you believe me?"

"It all makes perfect sense to me. I know my niece and I know Jake. Besides, I can't imagine anyone making up a story like that."

I felt like an anchor had just been cut loose from my heart.

"What's your name?" she said.

"Victoria Dowling."

"Call me Miss Theresa. Well, Victoria, I told you I know my niece. If she gave you my phone number, she's hoping you'll bring him here sooner or later. She'll want him back."

The anchor feeling suddenly came back. That was

another part of the story I'd left out. How The Hand had come back to the train, but it left the station, with me and Wills on it. "But she had no way of knowing who'd find him."

"You don't think so? Well, first things first. May I speak to Danny, please?"

"He's right here. He's asleep, though."

"I can't tell you how much it would ease my mind to talk to that little boy."

"Okay. Hold on."

I set the phone down and gently rubbed William's back. "Hey, buddy. There's someone on the phone for you."

Wills blinked, and then he sat up. The hair on one side of his head was damp with sweat, and he had lines on his cheek from my T-shirt. He had no idea where he was.

"It's okay, buddy. I can't really believe we're here either. Here—phone for you."

He looked up at me, and then he took the phone.

"'Lo?"

Suddenly he smiled the biggest smile I'd ever seen.

"Hi! Hi, Tee!"

If I hadn't been sitting on the ground already, I would've fallen over.

Wills talked for about a minute. Well, mostly he just listened with this huge smile on his face. Once he pointed to me and nodded and said "Sunshine." Then he said, "'Bye, Tee," and he gave the phone back to me.

"Tee," he said, still smiling.

"So I heard." I put the phone to my ear again. "Hello?"

"Hello, Victoria," said Miss Theresa. "Danny sounds just fine. Thank you for taking such good care of him."

She was thanking me. I had nabbed her beloved grand-nephew and hauled him halfway across the country without anyone's permission, and *she* was thanking *me*.

"You're—thank you too," I stammered. "Miss Theresa?"

"Yes?"

"Why did you think I was from Family Services?"

"Victoria, your instincts were right. Sandra Jean is a troubled young woman. I don't know how many times I've gotten calls from Family Services, telling me she left Danny alone for the night, or that Jake came around noisy drunk and the neighbors were complaining. I've begged her to let me have that child and be done with it. I even moved up from Tennessee to be near them. But she won't hear of it. And as long as Danny isn't hurt badly enough, the authorities won't take him away from her. I suppose I'm expected to wait until it's too late before anything can be done about it."

Suddenly I realized what she was saying. She knew that Wills was falling through the cracks.

"I'm sorry, dear," she said when I hadn't said anything for a minute. "I didn't mean to upset you."

"No, it's okay. I guess I sort of knew all that already. But wait—do you mean you want him permanently?"

"Since the day he was born. But he's not mine to keep. Sandra Jean will come for him, like she always does. It's just a matter of time."

I didn't like what I was hearing. "But why? He's not safe with her. She's a terrible mother. She doesn't love him."

"Now just one minute," said Miss Theresa. "Of course she loves him. I won't make excuses for her, Victoria. You know the Golden Rule, don't you? Treat others the way you wish to be treated? Well, it goes both ways: as you are treated, so you learn to treat others. Sandra Jean has never seen any other kind of mothering. Do you understand what I'm saying?"

"I think so." She was saying that Sandra Jean had fallen through the cracks herself. I felt bad for her, but did she have to pull Wills down with her?

Miss Theresa continued. "When someone like Jake comes along—someone who always has money in his pocket and can keep her in food and rent—she doesn't care how he treats her or where the money comes from. She just does what he tells her. He says no one will suspect that a young girl with a baby is shuttling drugs out of New York and cash back in, and so far he's been right. But one of these days she'll get caught."

"Wait a minute," I said. "When Jake 'comes along'? Isn't he Danny's father?"

"Heavens no," said Miss Theresa. "Jake showed up about six months ago. Bad news, that man. At least when Sandra Jean comes into the city, she brings Danny here to Brooklyn and I can take care of him for a few days."

So Jake had lied to the police about being Wills' father. Which made me mad, but it was also a relief. And the eight hundred dollars was drug money, which just made me plain old mad.

"Maybe she will get caught," I said. "She and Jake will get arrested, and go to jail, and they'll *have* to give you custody of Wills."

"That's a sad thing to hope for, isn't it?" she said. "But

I do admit it's crossed my mind, even though the thought of turning in my own niece gives me no peace. I've never seen any evidence, though, besides the cash, and you can't prove where cash comes from. Besides, even though it might help Danny now, he'd still lose his mother."

I closed my eyes. Any way you looked at it, we were screwed.

"The only reason I'm telling you all this, Victoria, is to help you understand things a little better. It's not an excuse, it's just an explanation. I'm sure you know there are no easy answers. Sandra Jean is not a very good mother. Still, she *is* Danny's mother. She loves him, and she takes care of him the best way she knows how."

I shook my head, as if somehow it would help me think better.

"I'm sorry Sandra Jean has had a hard life," I said, because I really was. "But why should the same thing happen to Wills? Isn't there something you can do to help him?"

"I don't know what more I can do. I can't say it any plainer. Sandra Jean is Danny's mother. And if she wants Jake in her life, I'm sorry to say there's nothing I can do about that either."

I had to lie down on the grass. I felt like I'd been knocked down.

"You can't stay away forever, Victoria. You're just postponing the inevitable."

"So then make it *not* inevitable!" I glanced around to see if anyone was watching. "I'm sorry," I said more quietly. "Please, Miss Theresa. There must be something we can do. What if I change my demand? I'll say that we'll come back if they give *you* permanent custody. Why can't *you* be his foster home?"

"If they could, I think they would give him to me. But I told you. He already has a mother."

"I can't believe you're just giving up on him like this!"

"Young lady, don't you think I've tried every way I know how to get custody of that little boy? And I'm blood family. If they won't listen to me, why would they listen to you? Now, I'm glad you were the one to find Danny in the first place, and you're taking good care of him now. Your heart is in the right place, but you won't be able to accomplish what you want here. You can't run forever. And if a child's mother says she wants him, as long as she keeps from breaking any of his bones, there's no way Family Services will take him away from her permanently. That's all there is to it."

I felt like I'd been slapped in the face.

"But—"

"I'm sorry," she said. "It's a harsh truth. It breaks my heart every bit as much as it breaks yours."

I knew every word she said was true. But knowing it didn't make it any less cruel.

"Listen to me, Victoria," Miss Theresa said. "Danny spends lots of time here. We can be grateful that Sandra Jean leaves him with me most nights she's in New York, which is most nights. That's better than nothing, isn't it? Now please—bring my baby on home. I'll meet you at Penn Station if you'd like. I'll be right there to take him into my arms. I can help you explain everything to the authorities."

"But they won't let you keep him, will they?"

"I honestly can't say. I wish I could make you that promise, but I can't."

That was the whole problem. "Why can't you? Why am I the only one who's willing to keep my promises?"

Miss Theresa sighed. "Maybe because the rest of us have learned not to make promises we can't keep."

"I'm sorry," I said, trying to sound like I was *not* losing it. "I *will* keep my promise."

"You're planning on running forever, then?"

"I don't know … " I said. Because I just didn't know.

"All right, Victoria. I know you're upset. And Lord knows I can't drag you home. Why don't you think things over? I hope you'll decide to bring him home, and if you do, I'll make you a promise I *can* keep. I promise to be there to meet you."

"Are you going to call the police?"

"What would you do if you were in my place, Victoria? Now, you seem to be a good girl, and it's obvious you're protective of Danny. But you're only fifteen. I'm wondering who's going to take care of you."

I didn't have an answer for that one.

"Victoria, listen to me. I don't want to make things harder for you, but I want my baby home. You need to do some hard thinking. Call me in a little while and we'll talk again. It's 12:30 now. Let's say you call me by two o'clock, all right? But if I don't hear from you by two o'clock, I'll be on the phone to the police and the FBI and anyone else I can think of. Do you understand?"

I understood perfectly. Too perfectly. "Yes, ma'am," I whispered.

"Good. And you take care of my Danny, now."

"I promise."

"I believe you, honey," she said, her voice softening again. "One more thing, Victoria. If you know his name is Danny, why do you call him Wills?"

I was glad she couldn't see me blush.

"I didn't know his name right away. I wanted to call him something, and William just popped into my head. Wills for short. He doesn't seem to mind."

Miss Theresa let out a short laugh. "Honey, you keep being sweet to him and I believe he'd let you call him Potato. Two o'clock, now."

"Yes, ma'am," I said. "Two o'clock."

 SIXTEEN

The Grand Canyon trip three years ago had been our last hurrah. Our last vacation as a real family.

The next summer, Dad said he was so exhausted from going back and forth to New York every day that he had no energy left, even for vacation.

But there was something else going on. Something no one was talking about.

"We don't have to go far," I offered one night when Dad was actually home for dinner. "We could drive to Maine like we did a few summers ago. We could finally take kayaking lessons. It'd be fun."

Dad smiled, but it wasn't a happy smile. "That does sound like fun, honey. And we'll do that one of these days,

I promise. But right now, even the thought of driving for five hours sounds like no vacation at all."

"Besides," said Mom, "By now every motel will be booked. You need to plan months in advance if you want to stay anywhere near the water." She didn't sound too broken up over it.

"What about Cape Cod, then?" I said. "It's less than three hours to the Cape. We could ride the ferry to Martha's Vineyard—"

Mom scraped her chair backward and stood up, tossing her napkin onto the table. She looked like she was going to cry.

"Mom?"

"The truth is, Victoria," said Dad, "I'm going to have to spend a lot of time in the city this summer. In fact—" he coughed—"I'll probably need to stay in the city most weeks this summer."

Now I stood up. "What? Why? You never said anything before. The whole summer? What about our vacation?"

"Honey, it can't be helped," said Dad, reaching for me. "I don't want to make a promise I can't keep."

I stepped away and looked over at Mom. "Someone tell me what's going on. You hate each other, don't you? I can tell. You never hug anymore, or smile. You argue about everything."

"Of course we don't hate each other," said Dad in a voice that said I was being ridiculous. But he wouldn't look at me when he said it. "I admit, this commuting to the city has taken its toll on all of us. If I can catch up on my work for a few weeks, then things will ease up, maybe."

And in that tiny little hesitation before the word "maybe"—in that infinitesimal fraction of a second—he gave himself away and I finally figured it out. And the voices flooded into my brain, as real as they had been the summer before at the rim of the Grand Canyon.

"Don't ever let go, Daddy."

"Never, baby girl. Never in a million years."

That perfect, happy moment—that achingly beautiful sunset that I'd wished would never end—was gone forever, and I knew it.

He was letting go.

"You're moving to New York, aren't you, Dad?"

He looked as if his heart were breaking. But I didn't care. He had caused his own broken heart, and mine too.

"It's just temporary, honey. Just to make things easier for a while."

Mom wheeled around and squeezed her hands into fists. "She's not stupid, Michael. The least you can do is be honest with her."

I glared at her. "So you knew about this too? When were you going to tell me?"

"Honey, we didn't want to say anything until we knew for sure," said Mom, her voice barely under control. "I don't think *we* even knew for sure, until just now." She and Dad looked at each other, and something in that look sealed the deal.

"Great," I said. "*Now* you agree on something."

And I walked out of the kitchen, leaving my old life behind forever.

↔ ↔ ↔

Dee-deet.

"'Lo? Tee?"

I sat up straight and shook myself alert. Had I fallen asleep? For how long?

"Let's see who it is," I said, rubbing my face and checking the caller ID.

It was Dad. The World Champion Breaker of Promises.

I took a deep breath, trying to get back into kidnapper mode. Then I punched the *talk* button.

"Now what, Dad?"

"Finally! I've been trying to call you back for over an hour." He was still in Dad mode. "Where are you?"

I was so not in the mood. "Hmmm. Ask me another question."

"Okay, how about if I answer it for you? Hall County, Georgia."

I almost dropped the phone.

"Victoria, Amtrak keeps records. You bought a ticket to Atlanta. And your cell phone's been traced to Georgia too. The police can do that, you know. They can trace your phone's signal to the nearest cell tower."

So they'd figured it out. "Dad—"

"Victoria, what in God's name are you thinking? Do

you know what this *means?* And your mother—she's already frantic. When she hears this—"

"Dad, please—"

"Enough. The Hall County Sheriff's Department has been directed to bring you and the baby back to New York. Do you hear me?"

My ears heard it, but my brain was having trouble keeping up. I glanced at Wills, who'd dozed off again, and then toward the courthouse.

Dad didn't wait for an answer. "Find a police officer and turn yourself in. Tell them it was all a big mistake and you want to come home. Officer Martinez has been working his tail off all night, making custody arrangements for Danny. You have no reason not to come home."

My brain finally kicked into gear. If Dad knew we were in Georgia, and the police knew, that meant—

"Does Jake know where we are?"

"The baby's father? Of course he does," said Dad. "The police have been keeping both of us apprised of the situation since yesterday."

"He's not the baby's father, Dad."

"What makes you say that?"

My heart was pounding. "Because he's *not.* Where is he now?"

"He's right—" and then Dad paused. "No, wait. He left. He said something about urgent business he had to take care of."

"When?"

"I don't know, maybe an hour ago. What does that have to do with anything?"

"Dad—I gotta go." I hit the *end* button and then *off*.

I sat for a minute, stunned. Then my mind raced.

How long would it take Jake to get to Georgia—ten or twelve hours by car? Or would he fly? How long would that take? He'd already gotten an hour's head start.

And apparently the police still bought his Upstanding Citizen act, so once he got here they'd bring him right to us. Because now they knew where to look.

I felt sick.

"Why is Jake doing this?" I asked Wills, but he was snoring again. "He doesn't care about you. Why is he going so crazy? You'd think it was a million dollars instead of eight hundred."

I thought again about the torn paper sack in Sandra Jean's canvas bag. With the stacks of bills, and the loose hundreds.

"Loose hundreds?"

I checked the stack in my pack. It didn't have any hundreds, only twenties. And there'd been more than one stack of money inside that paper sack. Two, or three, or maybe four, for all I knew. In all the panic and confusion at the time, I hadn't really bothered to count.

So what happened to the rest of the money?

A picture flashed in my mind—of Jake, on the platform at Penn Station, shaking the empty paper sack.

Slowly, I pulled my backpack toward me. One by one, I started emptying pockets.

I pulled out diapers, T-shirts, magazines, bus and train schedules, and a crumbled, linty cracker, and piled it all on the grass in front of me. But I didn't find any more money.

"This doesn't make sense," I said to myself, rechecking every compartment and finding nothing. "Why would he hunt us down for eight hundred dollars? Unless he's just totally insane." Which was a definite possibility. I turned my backpack over and over, making sure I hadn't missed any zippers.

"Wait a minute ... what's this?" It wasn't a compartment, exactly. And it had no zippers.

On the back of my pack, under the straps, was a padded liner—a wide flat pad that cushions your back from the stuff inside the pack.

That cushion was only partially attached to the back. There were slits at the sides, so you could tuck the straps down inside the cushion, and carry the pack by the top handle like a little suitcase.

I slid my hand inside the liner, and down into the bottom of the cushioned opening. And felt paper. Lots of paper.

"Holy crap," I breathed.

I jiggled Wills gently. "Come on, buddy," I whispered. "Wake up."

↔ ↔ ↔

A few minutes later we were back in the laundromat, in the little washtub room, with the door locked.

I sat cross-legged on the concrete floor next to Wills, with my backpack on my lap. "Ready?" I said to him.

He blinked up at me and yawned. I held my breath and pulled out the paper.

Sure enough. Cash.

I pulled out another stack, and then the hidden compartment behind the cushion was empty. There were two stacks of bills, each wrapped with rubber bands and about half an inch thick. Just thick enough to fit snugly under the cushion without shifting or feeling lumpy.

"Moneys?" said Wills, picking up a stack.

"Yeah," I breathed. "Lots of moneys."

That explained what had happened to the rest of Jake's money. I flipped through the stacks. They were all hundreds. Two stacks of hundred-dollar bills, maybe fifty bills in each stack.

"Fifty times a hundred is five thousand … five thousand times two is … "

"More moneys?" said Wills, reaching for the stacks.

"Yeah, I'll say. Ten thousand moneys. At least."

I sat. I stared. I blinked. I stared some more.

"Okay … " I said. "So Jake's not crazy. Definitely not crazy. It's very reasonable to want your ten *thousand* dollars back!"

The little windowless washroom had suddenly gotten very stuffy.

"Air," I said. "I need air." But when I stood up I felt lightheaded. I leaned over the sink and doused my face with cold water until the urge to barf went away.

"Moneys," Wills said again, confirming that I hadn't imagined the whole thing.

"Let's not talk about the moneys anymore, okay?"

He looked up at me and smiled. I wished I were feeling better, because I really wanted to try out "Potato" on him.

I crammed the stacks back inside the cushion of my backpack, tucking them in snug and deep. Then I sifted through all the junk I'd piled on the floor.

"Hey, buddy. Did you see where I put those train schedules?"

SEVENTEEN

I had two train schedules and a bus schedule. I jammed them all into my back pocket. Then I stuffed everything else into my backpack, picked up Wills, and headed out of the laundromat and into the hot sunshine.

"Eat?" Wills said, wiggling in my arms.

"Oh, crap. It's lunchtime, isn't it?" Right on cue, the clock tower chimed one o'clock.

"Okay, we'll make a quick pit stop, but then we have to cruise."

Instead of crossing the open town square, we walked along the sidewalk, in the shade. I didn't want to attract the attention of anyone sherrify.

The coffee shop was packed. People were talking and

laughing and clinking silverware and way too busy to notice two kids who by now were probably on the Universe's Most Wanted list.

"Can we get some sandwiches to go?" I asked the lady behind the counter as I slid onto the last empty stool.

"Oh, sure," she said, handing me a menu. "What would you like?"

I set Wills on my lap and showed him the menu. "What'll it be, Your Highness?"

"No," he said, pushing it aside. "Eat."

"I know that. But what do you like?" I pointed at the menu. "How about this? You liked the eggs at breakfast this morning."

"No. Eat."

I looked up at the lady. "Can we have two egg salad sandwiches on white bread, and some chips? To go?"

"Why sure," she said, smiling and making silly faces at Wills. "Ain't he a cutie. He your little brother?"

"Yep," I said, not missing a beat. "We're just spending the afternoon together."

She didn't miss a beat either. "Y'all don't look anything alike." She tickled Wills under his chin and raised her voice to a squeaky pitch. "No siree, you shore don't!"

I could feel my cheeks getting hot. I blurted out, "He's my half brother. My parents were divorced awhile ago, and my dad remarried." I lowered my voice and leaned closer to her. "Trophy wife." I rolled my eyes.

"Ahhh," said the lady, her face flooding with comprehension. She nodded and patted my hand.

"Well, I think it's lovely that the two of you are getting to know one another. There's all kinds of families. Do I know your daddy?"

"No . . . ." I was kind of sorry to disappoint her.

"Oh, I didn't think so," she said, waving her hand. Then she turned back to Wills and started flirting with him again. "Y'all ain't from around here, are you?"

Before I could think of what to say next, a booming voice spoke up from the other end of the counter.

"Hey now, Miss Ruthie," the voice said. "How about you quit scaring little kids and refill my tea glass?"

Miss Ruthie turned in the direction of the voice and gave a salute. "Yes sir, Deputy Tolliver. Icy cold sweet tea coming right up." Then she looked back at us and winked. "These'll be ready in just a minute." She wrote TO GO in big letters across the order slip and passed it through the window that opened to the kitchen behind her. Then she picked up a pitcher of iced tea and walked to the other end of the counter.

I leaned back on the stool as far as I could without being obvious or falling off.

There were five people between us and Deputy Tolliver, so I couldn't see his face. I did see a tan shirt, a wide rear end wearing dark brown pants, and a mostly bald, sunburnt head. A radio was clipped to his belt, and something else was sticking out on the other side. It could have been a gun.

Well howdy, Deputy. Fancy meeting you here, right

across the square from the courthouse. What are the chances?

I turned away from him as casually as I could. Not too fast. Not too slow. I resisted the urge to just get up and go, but only because Wills was reaching for the basket of sugar packets.

"Eat!" he insisted.

"Shhh," I whispered in his ear. "Pretty soon."

I pulled the bus and train schedules out of my pocket and spread them open on the counter. I figured if I couldn't see what Deputy Tolliver was doing, he couldn't see what I was doing. Besides, I could hear his loud voice, and he sounded too busy joking with Miss Ruthie to be concerned with anything else.

"Book?" said Wills, picking up the bus schedule.

"Not exactly," I said to him. "Gainesville isn't such a safe place after all." I studied the schedules, trying to find the quickest escape. I was half-tempted to turn myself in to the police. But what if Jake showed up? I'd be in the slammer, he'd launch into his Forlorn Father act, and the police would hand Wills over to him.

"Hey, this might work," I whispered into William's ear, pointing to the bus schedule. "There are buses leaving for Greenville every hour, and Greenville is also on the train line. So once we get there, if we need to make another quick getaway, we can still hop on a train. That should throw Jake off our trail."

"Order up!" called a voice from the kitchen, and a brown paper sack came sliding out from behind the window. Miss Ruthie delivered the sack and collected my money.

"Excuse me," I said. "How far is the bus station from here?"

"Not far. One block over and three blocks down." She nodded out toward the sidewalk. "Here you go, sugar," she said to Wills, handing him a red lollipop. He grabbed it like he was dying of hunger.

"Thanks," I said, folding the schedules and stuffing them and the paper sack into my backpack.

As we were going out the door, I heard the crackle of a two-way radio, and Deputy Tolliver's voice booming over the crowd. "Say again, Sheila? What's that APB? A couple of runaways?"

My heart pounded and I froze in the doorway.

"I got it. Just give me a minute. I got a hot plate of barbeque in front of me here. Call over to Betsy at the train station and tell her not to sell any tickets to any kids. They ain't going anywhere."

I had to admire a man who had his priorities straight. Lucky for us, Deputy Tolliver's priority was food. We started walking, and when we got past the windows of the coffee shop, I picked up Wills and ran.

By the time the deputy finished his hot plate of barbeque, we'd already be one block over and three blocks down.

↔ ↔ ↔

I felt like my lungs didn't know how to breathe the thick hot afternoon air. By the time we got to the bus station Wills and I were both dripping wet, and if we didn't eat those egg salad sandwiches in about two minutes they'd sprout stuff that would make any biology teacher proud.

But I couldn't slow down yet. I walked up to the ticket window.

"I need the next bus to … " I caught my breath and checked the schedule once more. " … to Greenville, South Carolina."

"That'll be $28.85," said the pimply-faced guy behind the window, without bothering to look at me. Then he waved his hand in the general direction of behind me. "That's it right there. Leaves at 1:45."

I pushed the money at him and glanced at my watch. Fifteen more minutes and we'd be out of reach of Deputy Tolliver. And Jake. And I had just enough time to call Miss Theresa. "Can we get on board now?"

He shrugged. "Yeah. Sure. I guess."

"Thanks," I said, but what I thought was, "don't quit school, buddy."

The bus was already running, and the air conditioning was on. Heavenly.

Wills and I walked toward the back and sat down. I slouched down in the seat and unwrapped the egg salad sandwiches. They were delicious. And nice and squishy, as Wills demonstrated.

"Chips?" said Wills.

I opened the bag for him and then settled back and closed my eyes.

But only for a second. I had just one more thing to do. I sat up straight and lifted my backpack off the floor.

"Time to call Miss Theresa," I said out loud.

"Tee?" said Wills, spraying a small blast of chip crumbs.

"Right. Deputy Tolliver was easy to lose, but if we don't call her before two o'clock we'll be dealing with the FBI."

I reached down for my pack, and then stopped.

"But what happens if I call Tee, and then Dad calls while I'm on the phone? Or Jake? Will they be able to trace the call even if I don't answer it?"

Wills gave up on the backpack and decided to hunt for treasure under the bus seats.

"If we call from here, before the bus leaves, we won't be giving them any new clues, will we? We're still in Gainesville. Anyway, we promised Miss Theresa."

I dug my phone out of my backpack and turned it on with one hand, while I grabbed the back of William's overalls with the other hand so he wouldn't crawl his way to the front of the bus.

The phone gave off a quiet little *beep*. The screen read *4 missed calls*. I shook my head and pressed the *clear messages* button. The phone gave off another little *beep*.

Wills crawled out from under the seat and stood up.

"Tee?" he said, reaching for the phone.

"Can I talk first, please?" I said, holding it out of his

reach. He pouted at me. I stuck my tongue out at him. He giggled.

I hit the *redial* button and waited while the phone rang at the other end.

"Hello?"

"Miss Theresa, it's Victoria."

"Thank you for calling back. Have you made any decisions?"

"The thing is … " I said. "Things have changed and I don't know if—"

Beep.

There it was again.

My heart jumped. Someone was beeping in. I closed my eyes tight, then peeked at the screen, wondering whose phone number I'd see there, glowing all blue and waiting.

But the screen didn't show anybody's number, or even *Unknown Caller*.

It said *low battery*.

And then it went blank.

EIGHTEEN

"Are you *kidding* me?" I said out loud. People turned around and glared at us. I slid low into the seat and my face burned.

"Tee?" said Wills. I gave him the useless phone, and he held it to his ear. "'Lo?"

"This can't be happening!" I whispered. "How could this be happening?" And since I'd very recently emptied out all the contents of my backpack, I knew I'd left the charger at home.

"I can't even plug in and call when we get off the bus. This phone is totally useless. How could I be so stupid?"

I wanted to scream. And suddenly that bus was hot and noisy and claustrophobic and I wanted to get off, just so I could breathe. But just then, the engine revved. A blast of blue exhaust floated past my window as we pulled out and headed for South Carolina. We were stuck.

"Now what?" I said. "I hope Miss Theresa doesn't think I just hung up on her. Does that count toward keeping my promise?"

Wills pushed the phone at me. "Tee?"

"It doesn't work, buddy," I said, shrugging and shaking my head. "See? Nothing happens when I push the buttons. No light or anything."

His lip started to quiver and his eyes watered. "Tee," he insisted.

"I'm sorry," I said. "It's broken. No Tee."

A sharp little whine welled up in the back of his throat and he threw the phone onto the seat.

"Please don't cry. Tee is still there. She's just not on the phone."

All he wanted was his Tee. I could give him that. But instead, I'd dragged him across nine states plus the District of Columbia. There were cops all the way from New York to Georgia trying to find him. All because of me.

"But they won't let her keep you," I told him, desperate to make him understand. Desperate to make myself believe I was doing the right thing. "Or what if Jake finds you first? You'll end up right where you started. At the edge of a huge crack, ready to fall in."

One big tear slid down his cheek. The whining noise got louder.

"I was just trying to protect you. I got scared. How

did we end up on a smelly hot bus in the middle of no-where, a zillion miles from home?"

Wills kept whining. Then he laid back his head, opened his mouth and wailed.

"Don't cry," I said, scooping him up and holding him tight. "Please don't cry. You'll make me cry, too." I rocked him and tried to ignore all the people making faces at us. Finally I whispered in his ear, "I want to go home too."

But it wasn't that easy. Even if Miss Theresa kept her promise and met us at Penn Station, how would I ever be able to keep my promise to Wills? I couldn't protect him from Jake.

I reached down and slipped my hand inside my back-pack's secret compartment. The money was still there, snug and tight.

Ten thousand dollars. Sandra Jean must've stashed it in my pack when I ducked into the bathroom on that first train. But why? She knew Jake would go off the deep end when he couldn't find it. And that he'd want it back.

Maybe she just didn't want to be caught with it. But she could've thrown it out the window, or flushed it down the toilet for real. Why did she saddle me with all that money?

Wills snuffled loudly and whimpered. I held him close and rocked him. He still smelled like baby shampoo. Out-side the window, fields of plowed orange dirt rolled by, row after row after row. A billboard announced *JESUS IS LORD AT THE PINE TREE MOTEL.*

"What, nowhere else?" I wondered out loud.

Okay, maybe I wasn't quite handling things as well as I'd thought. For example, it might've been a stupid idea to come this far. We probably could've gone back to New York and hidden out for ages. Who'd notice two kids in New York City? Ten thousand bucks could buy lots of Metro Cards. We probably could've ridden around in the subway for months and never be found.

"But now we're in Georgia," I said to Wills, wiping his nose with a napkin. "Or maybe South Carolina."

He blinked up at me. "Lina?"

"Maybe," I said. "But don't worry. At least now we're a little closer to home."

"Home?"

"You're not much of a conversationalist, are you?"

"Are you?" he echoed, and he took a couple of shuddering breaths. I turned him to face me on my lap, wiping his cheeks and his eyes with the hem of my shirt.

"That's okay," I said to him softly. "You're a good listener."

He blinked one last tear from his bottomless eyes.

"You have Magic Eight Ball eyes," I said. "Have you ever seen a Magic Eight Ball? You can find out if a boy likes you, or if you'll pass your math test, stuff like that. But one day I asked it if Mom and Dad would stay divorced forever, and it said, *Most likely.* So I threw it against the wall and it cracked. Did you know the liquid inside is blue? That stain still hasn't washed out of the carpet. Anyway, you ask the Eight Ball a question, and then you shake it a little, and the answer comes floating up out of the dark."

"Up?" said Wills with a little bounce.

"Right! So if I ask a question and look into your Magic Eight Ball eyes, will the answer float up for me to see?"

"See," said Wills, nodding.

"Okay, let's try it." I took his head in both my hands and closed my eyes. "Why did Sandra Jean put all that— you know—in my backpack?" I didn't want anyone to overhear me saying *ten thousand dollars*.

I jiggled Wills' head gently. He giggled.

"Hmmm . . . let's see here," I said, opening my eyes and gazing into his. He held perfectly still.

"*Better not tell you now.* That's no help, is it?"

Wills frowned and shook his head.

"I don't like it either," I told him. I was tempted to throw all that money out the bus window and let it blow across the rust-colored fields. It'd serve Jake right.

"Let's try another one." I closed my eyes. "Will Miss Theresa meet us at Penn Station like she promised? *If* we decided to go back to New York?"

I jiggled him. He giggled. We stared into each other's eyes.

"*It is decidedly so.* You know, I think that's right. I think we can trust Miss Theresa. Let's try another one."

I closed my eyes and held my breath for a second.

"Is it time to go back to New York?"

More jiggling and giggling.

"Hmmm . . . *Ask again later.*"

There were so many questions and no easy answers.

"Okay then, where's Jake?"

I stared into Wills' eyes and tried to think of a good Eight Ball answer, but the only thought that came into my head was *Cannot predict now.*

"That's the trouble. We don't know where he is, do we?"

"No," said Wills. Did he really understand what I was saying? It didn't really matter. It was someone to talk to.

"Let's try one more."

I closed my eyes again and a question popped out of my mouth. A question I hadn't even realized I was thinking until I heard myself asking it.

"Will either one of us live happily ever after?"

I opened my eyes and looked at Wills, his head in my hands. He waited and smiled. But I froze, and just stared into his eyes. I wanted to fall into those dark pools and sink to the bottom and stay there forever.

"I think it says, *Reply hazy try again.*"

He pulled my hands away from his head. Then he climbed over to the window and pressed his nose against the glass.

"Beeeg truck!" he said.

And suddenly, for the first time since this whole mess started, *happily ever after* sounded completely impossible.

What if Miss Theresa was right? What if I was postponing the inevitable? What if nothing I did—even something as desperate as kidnapping—made a single bit of difference?

Reply hazy.

And what if Dad was right? What if I'd screwed up my own future for a kid I'd never laid eyes on until yesterday?

Ask again later.

Wills and I had nothing in common, except one train ride and two really bad days. I didn't even know his last name. I'd told Dad that Wills and I needed the same things, and I still believed that—but not completely. Having two homes is *not* really the same as having no home at all. And it's nowhere near the same as having a home where you're in physical danger.

Maybe they all were right. Maybe I was being foolish and stubborn and stupid. Maybe I was in way over my head. Maybe nothing I did would keep Wills from falling through the cracks.

Maybe I *had* made a promise I couldn't keep.

But Jake had made promises of his own. I had his pictures and videos and text messages in my cell phone to prove it. And now he was out there somewhere, looking for us. *Outlook not so good.*

"Sunshine?" William's head was cocked to one side, as if he wanted to know what I was thinking about.

"Know what I'm thinking?" I whispered. "I think I really hate that Magic Eight Ball."

NINETEEN

It was almost five o'clock when we got to Greenville. We stumbled off the bus, squinting in the sunshine, and went to change Wills' diaper. We were getting that routine down pretty good.

"Okay," I said when we were done. "We need to call Tee again. I wonder if she's called out the National Guard yet." Then I forced myself to sound happy. "Are you ready to say hi to Tee?"

Wills nodded and hopped. "Tee."

A pay phone hung on the outside wall of the bus station. I dug out all my loose change and dumped it on the little shelf under the phone. Then I pulled out the magazine where I'd copied Miss Theresa's phone number, checked the number, and dialed.

"Hello?" a voice answered.

"Miss Theresa? It's Victoria again."

"Victoria, what happened? We were cut off earlier."

"I know. I'm sorry. My cell phone died and I had to wait until I could find a pay phone." I swallowed hard. "Have you—called the police?"

"Not yet. I've been hoping you've decided to come home. Are you all right? You sound different. Is Danny all right?"

I stood up straight and cleared my throat.

"He's fine. I'm fine. Everything's fine. Do you want to say hi to him?"

"Yes, please."

I gave Wills the phone and they chatted. He got that huge grin again. I had to look away.

After a minute, Wills held the phone out for me, and then scrunched down to inspect a line of ants on the ground.

"Now," said Miss Theresa, "have you thought any more about coming home?"

"I've thought about it," I said. "I really wish we could come home…"

"Of course you do, Victoria. Don't you think that would be a wise choice?"

My choices were jail, or Jake, or both. What kind of choice was that?

"I'm sorry, Miss Theresa. I made a promise to Wills

—to Danny. We can't come home if it means breaking that promise."

"Young lady—" She was finally starting to sound exasperated. "This has to end sometime. I'm afraid that if you don't come home on your own, I'll have to—"

"No," I said, fighting back panic. "No, Miss Theresa, please don't. If you call the police, we'll just run in another direction. And we'll stop calling."

She didn't say anything.

"I'm really sorry," I said. "I feel so bad for saying that. But I mean it."

She sighed heavily. "Well, I'm sorry too. So what's next, Victoria? Where will you sleep tonight?"

Before I had time to think, I said, "The Pine Tree Motel." I shut my mouth tight before I could add, "Where Jesus is Lord." Although for half a second I wondered if that might make her feel better.

Then I said, "Don't worry. I have enough money. And I'll die before I let anything happen to Wills."

"Let's hope it doesn't come to that," said Miss Theresa. "You know, eight hundred dollars might sound like a lot of money, but it won't last as long as you think."

I wanted to tell her about the ten thousand dollars. I wanted to tell *somebody*. But that would put her into a panic for sure. Instead I said, "We'll be all right."

Just then, Wills disappeared around the corner of the building. I gasped out loud.

"Victoria?" said Miss Theresa. "What is it?"

"Hold on," I said, dropping the phone receiver. It

bounced at the end of its cord as I nabbed Wills and led him back around to where I could see him.

"Handful and a half," I muttered, pulling his toy truck out of the bag for him and sitting him on the ground. "Play with this."

I picked up the receiver again.

"Miss Theresa?"

"I'm here," she said. "What happened?"

"Uh—Wills was getting bored. He's okay now."

"Victoria, I told you to think hard about all this. What do you think Sandra Jean meant for you to do, once you found Danny?"

"What? She didn't mean for me to do anything," I said. "She had no way of knowing *who* would find him. She *left* him."

"I'll agree it was a foolish, stupid thing to do," said Miss Theresa. "But didn't you tell me earlier that you watched the two of them pretty closely? Do you think Sandra Jean might have noticed that?"

The image came to me of Sandra Jean's face, just inches from mine. She'd had that weird look in her eyes, and she'd said those words: *You be careful.*

"Maybe…" I said.

"Let's say she did, for the sake of argument," said Miss Theresa. "Let's say she knew you were watching. So she made sure you'd have my phone number, and gave you enough money to get him to me. And then she left him before Jake showed up. Don't you think that adds up to more than coincidence?"

I didn't know what to say.

Miss Theresa didn't wait for an answer. "I do *not* think she wanted you to go all the way to Georgia."

My face burned.

"Sandra Jean wants you to bring Danny to me, Victoria," said Miss Theresa. "It's clear as day. And you're going against her wishes."

"I don't know," I said. "I—"

Wills pushed his truck around the corner of the building.

"I'm sorry, Miss Theresa," I said. "Wills is—I have to go. I'll call back soon." And I hung up and chased after Wills again.

He had followed the line of ants around the corner, and now he was running them over with his truck.

"So this is your idea of fun?" I asked.

"Bug," he said, pointing.

"Dead bug." I took his hand. "Come on. I have five bucks' worth of change sitting on the pay phone."

Was Miss Theresa right? Did Sandra Jean really try to tell me what she wanted me to do? But how could she be sure I'd do what she wanted?

I snorted. "I *didn't* do what she wanted. Well, it was a weird way to ask a favor. And why did she threaten me like that? *You be careful?*"

I sunk to the ground next to the phone and studied William's beautiful face. "You miss your Tee, don't you?"

"Tee? 'Lo?" he said, pointing up at the pay phone.

"I'm so sorry I got us into this. Honestly, I was trying

to do the right thing. Jake's out there somewhere. It seems like no matter what we do, we're going to lose."

I rubbed my eyes and forehead. Wills ran his truck up and down my leg.

"If I take you home, you'll fall through the cracks for sure. Even the police can't promise that won't happen. I wish I knew what to do. I'm not even sure where we are. I'm scared—"

I had to stop and take a deep breath. Then I looked into William's bottomless Eight Ball eyes.

"I'm scared of breaking my promise to you. It's a life-or-death promise."

And for the second time I remembered what Miss Theresa had said about making promises you can't keep.

I held out my arms, and Wills fell into them, all warm and soft. I held him and rocked him and buried my face in his neck.

"Sunshine?" he said, pulling away to look me in the eye. He kept his face so close, we were almost touching noses. Then he planted a kiss on my face, somehow managing to slobber me up even more than I was slobbering myself.

I couldn't help smiling. "You think my name is Sunshine, funny boy? Well, you're my sunshine, you know."

"No," he said. "Eat?"

"Okay, come on," I said, standing up and wiping my face. "Let's find you a snack. And then I guess we need to find out where the Pine Tree Motel is. One good thing about a dead cell phone—no one can trace it. We should be safe here for the night, anyway." I scooped up all the rest of my change and was about to put it in my pocket.

Then I stopped.

"Wait..."

"What!" said Wills.

"My cell phone. Jake's messages. The video and the pix..."

"Pix!"

"That's it! We have proof. We have *proof* that Jake is dangerous."

"Poof!" said Wills, going into his cheerleader bit.

"And the ten grand. That has to be proof of—something. That Jake and Sandra Jean are doing something illegal, right?"

"Eat?" said Wills, tugging my hand.

"Hold on." I turned around, spilled the change back onto the pay phone shelf, stuck coins into the slot, dialed Dad's cell phone, and waited.

As soon as I heard the click at the other end of the line I started talking. "Dad, listen, we're—"

"I'm not available right now," said Dad's recorded voice. "Leave a message."

I held my breath as I waited for the beep and then it all rushed out. "Dad, I have proof that Jake is dangerous. He made threats—they're saved in my cell phone. And I have ten thousand dollars in cash that he stole from someone. That's why he's looking for us. He's not Wills' father. He doesn't care about Wills. He wants his money. Tell Officer Martinez. We're coming home." And I hung up.

Then I smacked the receiver against the pay phone. "Voice mail? Where is he?"

Wills jerked at my arm again. "Eat!"

"God, I hope he gets that message. Did I make sense? Do you think he'll believe me?"

"Eat!" said Wills. "Eat eat eat!"

I gasped. "Oh, no! Jake's too smart. He's probably keeping in touch with the police, no matter where he is. Now he'll know we're coming home too!"

Wills plopped onto the ground and opened my backpack. "Eat!" he said. "Chips?"

"We need insurance," I said. "We need someone besides Miss Theresa on our side."

"No," said Wills, still digging.

Once more, I picked up a handful of change and plugged the phone. Then I dialed 411.

"Directory assistance," said the voice on the other end. "What city?"

"New York City . . . . I need the phone number of a TV or radio station. One of the big ones."

"I'm sorry, Miss. I need a name I can look up."

"Uh . . . W-something?"

"I'm sorry, Miss. You'll have to be more specific."

"I can't remember the exact name. Wait—how about a newspaper? The—*The New York Times*."

I heard tapping sounds on the other end.

"I have several listings for *The New York Times*," said the operator. She couldn't possibly have sounded more bored.

I ran my sweaty hand across my forehead. "I need a reporter. A reporter, I don't know what number that would be."

"I have Opinion Page, Features, News—"

"News!" I practically shouted. Then more quietly, "Yes. News."

"International, National, Regional, City Desk—" I was pretty sure she was enjoying this.

"City Desk!" I said, as if I'd just won a prize or something. "Is that the person who writes the front page?"

"I don't know, Miss. Would you like that number? Or I can connect you for fifty cents."

"Yes, connect me! Please connect me."

I plugged the phone with more change, and it rang on the other end. I forced myself to breathe evenly and got ready to sound convincing.

Finally a voice said, "*Times* City Desk."

"Hello—I need to talk to a reporter about that kidnapping in Penn Station yesterday. Do you know about that?"

"Hold on," said the voice, and then there was nothing for a few seconds. I hopped like I had to go to the bathroom.

Then another voice came on.

"George Silva here. You have information about the Penn Station kidnapping?"

"Yes," I said. "That little boy's life is in danger."

"What kind of danger?"

I let myself get slightly hysterical. "Horrible, HORRIBLE danger! A sweet, innocent, BEAUTIFUL little boy!

If you want to know more, be at Penn Station for the next train coming from Greenville, South Carolina."

"I'll think about it," said George Silva. "How do you know all this?"

I took a deep breath and held it for a second. Then I let it out.

"Because I'm the kidnapper."

 TWENTY

"Eat. Eeeeeeeeet!" insisted Wills as I hung up the phone, exhausted and excited at the same time.

"Okay, okay, okay," I said. "Now we can get a snack. Then we have to get busy. Do you think I convinced him with the 'horrible danger' thing? God, I hope this works!"

"Eat," said Wills.

We bought cookies and juice from the vending machines, and I sat him down on a bench to eat them. Then I dug the train and bus schedules out of my pack.

"Okay, now we have to get on a train and hope that George shows up at Penn Station," I said. "I remember seeing Greenville on one of these train schedules..."

Wills squished his juice box and the juice shot out the straw in an arc.

"You're so disgusting sometimes. Ha! Here it is."

I unfolded the schedule for the Amtrak Crescent—the train we'd ridden down from Newark in the first place.

Sure enough. The train turned around in New Orleans, and then went all the way back to New York along the same route. It would stop in Greenville at 7:00 that night and get to Penn Station at 10:12 the next morning. I checked my watch.

"Holy crap!" I said. "The train leaves in an hour! And we don't even know where the train station is. Come on."

We scrambled into one of the cabs idling at the curb in front of the bus station.

"How long does it take to get to the train station?" I asked the driver.

"Ten minutes or so."

I plopped back into the seat. "We'll have time to call Miss Theresa from the station. I can't wait to tell her we're coming home."

Wills was inspecting the contents of the cab's ashtray.

"Yuck." I pulled his fingers out. "Let's just make sure the train is on schedule and everything first, so we don't give her the wrong information." I laid my head back and closed my eyes. "At least we don't have to worry about where to sleep tonight. Hotel Amtrak." Although I was kind of disappointed that we wouldn't get to see if Jesus really was Lord at the Pine Tree Motel.

The Greenville train station was small but busy. There

was one ticket window at the far end of the room, and a bank of pay phones sat just inside the door.

I set everything down on the floor and gave Wills one of his books. Then I checked the schedule board for the Amtrak Crescent.

"There it is, right on time. Okay, ready to call Tee?"

"Tee," said Wills, engrossed in his book.

I dug a handful of coins out of my pocket and plugged the phone. By now I knew Miss Theresa's phone number by heart.

"Hello?"

"Miss Theresa? It's Victoria."

"Victoria? What's going on?"

"I've decided. We're coming home."

I thought I could hear her smile.

"Oh, my. I'm so happy to hear that."

I gave her the train information. "Can you—will you meet us there?" I asked, suddenly scared that she'd changed her mind.

"Didn't I promise you, darlin'?"

I nodded.

"Yes, ma'am," I said. "You did."

I hung up and looked at Wills.

"Guess what? In the morning, you're going to see your Tee!"

"Tee?" he said, and he smiled.

I scooped up the rest of my change and was about to put it in my pocket.

But instead, I stuck a few more coins into the slot

and dialed. And waited. And listened to the phone on the other end ring and ring and ring.

Finally someone answered.

"Hello?"

I took a deep breath.

"Mom? It's me."

"Victoria! Baby, where are you? Are you all right?"

"I'm okay, Mom," I said, ready to laugh and cry at the same time, just from the sound of her voice. "Mom—I'm coming home."

"Oh, thank God! I've been worried sick. Why haven't you been answering your phone? Are you sure you're all right? Is the baby okay?"

"Yes, Mom. We're both fine, but—"

I had to bite my lip for a second.

"Honey? What is it?"

"Mom—"

And then I just lost it. I started crying and couldn't stop.

"It's okay, honey," I heard her say quietly. "I'm here."

I guess I cried for a long time. The phone beeped in my ear once and I had to deposit two more quarters just so I could keep crying. Finally I cleared my throat.

"So you know about Wills?" I sniffed hard. "Do you know everything?"

"Dad called me as soon as it happened. I think I've been on the phone for twenty-four hours straight. The only reason I haven't gone down to New York or chased after you myself is the hope that you might show up here at home. Did you go to the police, like Dad told you to? Are they bringing you back? What on earth possessed you to go all the way to Georgia, anyway?"

"Mom, please. I don't have time—" I heaved a sigh. "No, I'm not with the police, my cell phone battery died, and we're getting on the train to New York in a few minutes. On our own. We're fine. We're safe. We'll be home in the morning."

"Oh, honey," she said. "Please just find a policeman and let him bring you home."

"Mom, no!" I pleaded. "I have to do it this way. We'll be fine."

She didn't say anything for a long time.

"Mom," I whispered. "Please."

Finally I heard her sigh, and I could breathe again.

"What can I do about it, anyway? You'd be halfway home before I could even catch up with you. Do you promise that you're getting on that train and coming straight to New York?"

"I promise, Mom. Thank you. But Mom?"

"Yes, baby?"

I swallowed hard. "Can you be there? Come meet my train?"

"Just tell me where and when. I'll be there."

↔ ↔ ↔

I wiped my face on my sleeve and gathered up all our stuff.

"Come on, buddy," I said, taking Wills' hand. "Let's go."

But before we got to the ticket window, I froze.

Would this work? My name was already in the Amtrak computer. When the ticket person entered my name this time, what would happen? Alarms? Sirens? Would the police come running?

I couldn't let that happen. Not now. We were so close to getting home on our own. And I'd just promised half the world that we'd be on this train. What would they think if we broke our promise now?

"No way," I said to myself. "Nothing can keep us from getting on that train now." Then I noticed something against the far wall. It looked like an ATM machine, but it had a big Amtrak logo on the side.

"What's that?" I said out loud.

"What?" said Wills. I picked him up and wandered over for a closer look.

"A ticket machine!"

Could it be that easy? Just punch a few buttons and get on the train, avoiding human contact completely? Can a machine ask to see your photo ID?

"You must have to put your name in somehow. Then what?"

Someone tapped my shoulder, and I jumped about six feet.

"Excuse me honey, you gonna use this machine right now?" said a lady.

"Oh. No. Go ahead." And I stepped aside to let her use it.

I turned away a little, but watched her out of the corner of my eye.

The lady touched the screen, working her way through the menus. It looked like she was selecting cities.

"Departure and destination," I whispered to Wills.

Then a keyboard appeared on the screen, and she touched a whole series of letters.

I swallowed. "Name," I whispered.

"Name," Wills whispered back.

Next, the lady slid a plastic card into a slot on the front of the machine.

"Credit card..."

The machine clicked and hummed, and in a few seconds a slip of paper fell into the hopper below the screen. The lady pulled it out, retrieved her credit card from the slot, and walked toward the tracks.

"What if we just get on the train and pay on board?" I wondered out loud.

"Board?" Wills answered.

"But they might be looking for two kids traveling alone. And they'd ask to see my ID for sure. The lady at the machine didn't scan her driver's license or anything. I think the machine might be safer."

A thought flashed in my brain, and I glanced up and around. I didn't see anything, but that didn't mean they weren't there. "We should decide quick. We don't need to be immortalized by Greenville surveillance cameras."

I sidled up to the machine and looked it over. "Crap," I breathed. "I don't see any slots for cash."

"Crap," said Wills, who was still playing the whispering game.

"Hey, no more bad words." I set Wills down on the floor and dug into my backpack. "You know what this means, don't you?"

"No," he answered.

"It's absolute desperate emergency time. Ah, here it is."

I pulled Mom's credit card out of my pack, took Wills by the hand, and stepped to the machine. I started working my way through the touch-screen menus, tapping on NEW YORK PENN when the destination choices appeared.

When the keyboard popped up asking for my name, I hesitated.

"The name on the ticket has to match the name on the ID, right?" I thought for a minute. "So ... how about this?"

I tapped on the keyboard and stepped back to admire my work.

First name: Tori.

Last name: Darling.

The slightly morphed names might just pass the customary quick-glance-at-the-ID test. But they also were different enough that the computer might not put two and two together, at least not right away. I could only hope.

I tapped my foot as I waited for the machine to do its clicking and humming thing. I grabbed my ticket from the hopper, jammed it into my back pocket, and we headed in the direction of the tracks.

"Hmm. That *was* easy... almost too easy. Oh well, whatever. As long as it gets us on the train, right?"

"Right," agreed Wills.

I checked the schedule board one more time to get the right track number, and we started cruising. It was funny how just yesterday we couldn't get far enough away from New York City. And today, we couldn't get back there fast enough. All I wanted was to be home.

"Just a minute there!" a deep voice called from behind us. From the direction of the ticket machine.

I stopped. But I couldn't turn around. I could hardly breathe. And all I could think was that sure enough, it *had* been too easy.

I hugged Wills tight. "Maybe he's not talking to us," I whispered. My feet started moving again.

"Miss!" called the voice. "Hold up there."

Okay, so maybe he *was* talking to us.

"This can't be happening," I breathed into Wills' ear. "Not now. Can't they just let us get home?"

I heard footsteps, and then they stopped, and the person with the deep voice was standing right behind us.

"Hi," said Wills, as if everything was just peachy.

"Hey, little man," said the deep voice.

There was nothing I could do. I turned around.

A large man in a uniform stood there. A security guard.

"Sorry, miss," he said. "I noticed you just used that ticket machine over there?"

My throat was too tight to answer. I nodded.

"I'm glad I caught you."

Caught. After I'd told Miss Theresa, and Mom, and *everyone* we were coming home. They'd all be waiting for us at Penn Station, and we wouldn't be there. And all I could think of was Miss Theresa warning me about making promises I couldn't keep.

The man put out his hand. I expected him to be holding handcuffs or something. But he was holding something else.

"You forgot this," he said. "Wouldn't want you walking off without it."

It was Mom's credit card.

I took it and blinked up at him. "Thanks," I squeaked.

"No problem." He smiled at Wills and held his hand out, palm up.

"How 'bout five, little man?"

Wills smacked the security guard's palm with his own hand and giggled.

"All right." He winked at Wills, and then he sauntered away.

"Ohhhh God. Can you have a heart attack when you're fifteen?"

"Bye!" said Wills, waving at the security guard.

I pulled his arm down and turned away. "Let's get on that train before something else happens."

 TWENTY-ONE

Ten minutes later, we were finally on our way home. Well, first I had to show my ticket and ID to a lady at the entrance to the platforms, but I flashed them quick and breezed through without a second glance. Without much of a first glance, for that matter. Which made me wonder which was the bigger threat to national security: terrorists, or minimum-wage security people? But right at that moment I didn't really care.

My seat-choosing Goldilocks mode kicked in, but after hauling Wills, my backpack, and the shopping bag full of toys through four train cars, I didn't care where we sat. People were hogging extra seats, spreading out for the overnighter on the train. Finally, I felt lucky to find two empty seats together. I grabbed them while we had the chance.

Poor Wills was so tired. He flopped over and put his head in my lap right away.

"Sunshine?" he asked.

I sang to him, forcing myself to sing slowly, hoping it would slow down my own heartbeat. My sweaty palms dampened Wills' hair. As I sang, I kept my eyes on the front door of the train car and my ears open for footsteps from behind. Would they be on the alert for a teenage girl and a two-year-old boy traveling alone together? That was definitely possible, since I'd just told pretty much the whole world that we'd be on this train.

But Wills and I would be together for only a few more hours. No one was going to cut that short now.

Careful not to wake him, I reached down and pulled two T-shirts out of my backpack. I covered William's legs with one shirt and his back with the other, leaving enough slack over his shoulders so that I could cover his head when the conductor came by. I got out my magazines and spread them around on top of Wills. Then I put my almost-empty backpack on top of his feet. I stuffed the bag of toys under the seat, and then I picked up a mag and held it open on my lap, about an inch above Wills' sleeping face.

As long as the conductor came by soon, and Wills didn't wake up, no one would even know he was there.

I hoped.

↔ ↔ ↔

I was so sleepy. But I was afraid to fall asleep until the conductor punched my ticket and we were safely on our way home. I held my breath every time I heard footsteps behind me, but still no conductor. After half an hour, I decided that the most luxurious thing in the whole world would be to move a little in my seat. But I was too scared even to shift my weight from one cheek to the other.

Finally, at 7:40 the conductor came through. I covered Will's head with the T-shirt and held the mag just above my lap. I pretended to read while I held up my ticket between my first two fingers.

The conductor got to my seat and stopped. I could see his shiny belt buckle out of the corner of my eye. He took my ticket and punched it, but he didn't hand it back. He just stood there.

"Going all the way to New York, miss?" he asked.

I glanced down at the pile of magazines on the seat next to me, hoping that I was the only one who noticed they were very gently breathing. I cleared my throat and forced myself to look up.

"Huh?"

He was looking right at me. But he just smiled and handed back my ticket.

"If you need anything before we get there, let me know."

"Oh. Thanks." I tried to smile back.

"You know, if you recline the seats and put some of that stuff in the overhead rack, the baby will have a little more room."

I must have looked as sick as I felt, because he frowned and said, "Something wrong?"

Yeah, something was wrong. I was stupid, that's what was wrong. Why had I risked something like this? With a zillion cops out hunting for us all up and down the Atlantic seaboard?

I croaked, "I didn't think I had to pay for him?"

The conductor's face relaxed. "Well, the little ones are free with their parent or guardian. Are you his parent or guardian?"

By now I was a seasoned kidnapper, so it was easy enough to look him square in the eye and say, "Yes. Yes, I am."

"Okay, then. You're all set here." He smiled again, and then he turned and walked up the aisle, calling for tickets. I held my breath until he passed through to the next car.

"Oh good grief," I whispered to myself, collapsing into my seat.

It wasn't even eight o'clock, but I was so tired. I put the magazines away, reclined our seats, and hoped that we'd both sleep for hours and hours, so that by the time we woke up we'd be almost home.

I started dreaming.

I dreamed that Wills and I were back at Penn Station, and we were standing in the doorway of the train.

Dad came marching along the platform, leading a

pack of policemen. He pointed at me and shouted, "There she is! I Spy . . . my kidnapper daughter!"

Suddenly there was a rumbling and everything shook, like an earthquake or something. The train lurched one way, and the platform lurched the other way. I looked down at the wide yellow line that marks the gap between the train and the platform, and watched it crumble and fall into a crevice that was opening below us.

Deputy Tolliver from Gainesville stepped to the edge of the crevice, with a big black gun in one hand and a barbecue sandwich in the other hand. Officer Martinez was next to him, smiling and nodding and holding a little cage for Wills. George the Reporter held up a huge old-fashioned camera with a light bulb that went *POP!* when he took our picture. Miss Ruthie from the coffee shop pushed through the crowd, waving a greasy paper sack. "Y'all forgot your egg salad, honey!"

The earth shook again, and the crevice between the train and the platform yawned wider. Beneath my feet there was nothing but blackness.

Sandra Jean ran up, and I thought she was going to drop right into the gaping hole. She stopped just in time, and yelled, "Be careful! Didn't I tell you to be careful?"

Then Mom was on the platform, her face all swollen and wet from crying. A sweet-faced old lady was there too, holding a phone in her hand. They both held out their arms, crying, "My baby!"

I'd have to jump across, before the gap got any wider and we'd be stuck on the wrong side forever.

Just then, Jake the Wall shoved everyone aside, growling, "Where's my money? Who said you could take that money?"

And before I knew what was happening, he reached across and grabbed Wills by the hand and yanked him. I held onto Wills as tightly as I could, but he slipped more and more, until I was holding him by his legs, and then by his feet, and he was stretched across the bottomless crevice, with me holding his feet and Jake pulling on his hands.

"You can't have him!" I yelled. "I made a promise!"

But Jake kept pulling, and I pulled back, and Wills slipped some more, and suddenly, all I was holding was a pair of empty shoes.

I looked up to see Wills swinging across the crevice toward Jake, who laughed and let go of William's hands.

"NO!" I screamed.

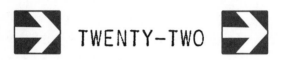 TWENTY–TWO

I jumped so high I woke myself up, and I almost knocked Wills off my lap. I put one hand on him to make sure he wouldn't roll onto the floor, and the other hand on my chest to keep my heart from pounding right through.

I took a few deep breaths. The lights in the train car were turned down, and most people were sleeping. It was one thirty in the morning.

Wills was completely uncovered now. I covered him up again with my T-shirts and tried to get comfortable and go back to sleep, but every time I closed my eyes I saw all those people coming at me, yelling and waving cages and guns and egg salad sandwiches. And Jake. And that dark, bottomless crevice.

I shook myself awake, to try and knock that horrible image out of my brain.

"I wonder if this was such a good idea after all," I whispered to myself. "But it's too late now. Everyone knows we're coming. We're being sucked into a vortex now, and there's nothing we can do about it."

My mind steered itself back to the dream. What had Sandra Jean said?

You be careful.

That's what she'd said to me on the first train, right before she got off without Wills.

Miss Theresa thought Sandra Jean knew I'd been watching them... and that she knew I'd look for Wills once she got off the train alone.

How did Miss Theresa know that? How could she be so sure that's what Sandra Jean meant?

And then Miss Theresa had said it was too much of a coincidence that Sandra Jean had given me a chunk of money, and took my phone number—right before leaving Wills on the train.

"That *is* a pretty wild coincidence," I whispered.

You be careful.

At the time, it had sounded like a threat. But now I wondered. Maybe it hadn't been a threat after all. Maybe it had been a warning. Was she warning me about Jake?

Then I remembered Dad, saying that Sandra Jean's story didn't match mine. But maybe it was like that surveillance video—maybe it all depended on how you looked at it.

But if I was supposed to keep Wills safe, then why did she give my phone number to Jake? And why did she saddle me with the ten grand?

I looked down at Wills. He was sprawled across the seat and my lap. And I was jittery and sweaty and I had to go to the bathroom.

"Oh, great," I whispered.

I tried to ignore it, but the more I tried to ignore it, the more I had to go.

"Okay, here's the deal," I whispered as I gently lifted Wills' head and slid out from under him. "I'll be right back."

I covered Wills with the T-shirts. Then I folded my sweatshirt and wedged it against him to keep him from rolling onto the floor. I tiptoed to the bathroom as quickly as I could, and closed the door.

Instantly, I got a flash of that first day—the way my heart had pounded when I pushed past The Hand and locked myself in the bathroom just before we got to Penn Station. The way she'd stared me down with her scared and defiant eyes. The way she'd leaned in close and said *You be careful.*

Suddenly I knew for sure it wasn't a threat. It wasn't a warning, either. It was a request. A plea.

"Wills," I told myself in the bathroom mirror. "She wanted me to be careful with Wills."

It all depended on how you looked at it.

It was like all the jumbled thoughts in my head were pieces of a jigsaw puzzle that were finally fitting into the right places. But the picture that was forming wasn't anything like the one I was expecting.

"Miss Theresa was right. Sandra Jean wanted me to find Wills in the bathroom. And she stuck the money in my backpack, so I could buy him food and diapers and get him safely back to Miss Theresa. Because...."

There was only one reason.

"Because she was scared of Jake."

She'd been asking for my help. To do what she couldn't do herself: to keep her little boy safe.

"Well, this is just wild," I said. "She was trying to protect Wills."

I looked myself straight in the eye.

"And she did, too."

Then I watched my own mouth drop open as I gasped.

"And I just left him alone!"

I yanked the bathroom door open and lurched back to my seat in a panic. I needed to see with my own eyes that Wills was still sleeping peacefully in the seat, just the way I'd left him.

But the seat was empty.

I swallowed a scream and double-checked. This was the right seat—my sweatshirt and T-shirts were still there. But no Wills.

I groaned and knelt down on the floor. I'd just figured out that his mother had entrusted him to my care, and I'd left him alone to fall onto the floor.

But he wasn't on the floor either.

"Wills?" I squeaked, dropping onto my stomach to get a better look under the seats.

No Wills. Only crumpled paper bags and scattered newspapers and feet with their shoes off.

I looked up and down the aisle.

Nothing.

I checked the seats all around me. Lots of grownups sleeping with their mouths open, but no Wills.

"Okay," I whispered to myself. "Don't panic. It's just dark in here, that's all. It's not a big train car. He couldn't have gone far. You were gone for only a minute. How could this happen so quickly? He was sound asleep when you left him. You'll find him. Don't panic."

Then I panicked.

The train car spun around me. I stumbled down the aisle, looking right and left and right and left until I was dizzy. I fought against the motion of the train, and it felt like one of those dreams where I'm trying to run as fast as I can, but my legs are as heavy as lead.

Then I saw all the suitcases piled in the baggage cubby at the back of the car, and I pushed toward it.

"Wills?" I hissed into the stack of suitcases. "Are you in there?"

No answer.

I yanked suitcases off the top of the stack with my sweaty hands, until I could see all the way to the floor.

He wasn't hiding there.

I dropped down onto my hands and knees, and crawled back up the aisle, looking under every single seat.

I was glad it was one thirty in the morning and no one could see me freaking out. I checked in the bathroom, in case he ducked in right after I came out. I even looked in the overhead racks.

No sign of Wills anywhere.

My stomach churned.

"How could you do this?" I yelled at myself silently. "You've been bragging to everyone that you can handle it. Dad, and Mom, and Miss Theresa, and Officer Martinez. You wouldn't go to the cops. You played cat and mouse with Jake. You were so sure you could do it all yourself. Sandra Jean asked you to keep him safe, and now look!"

I thought I was going to throw up right there in the aisle of the train car.

"Miss?" a voice behind me said.

I spun around. It was the conductor with the shiny belt buckle, and he was holding Wills in his arms.

"Wills!" I croaked, and I grabbed him and squeezed him hard.

"Sunshine," said Wills, squeezing me back.

"What happened? I got so scared! You just disappeared."

"We thought you were the one disappeared," said the conductor. He was smiling, but his eyebrows were scrunched together. "I came on through and found him sitting alone, crying for his mama. I thought maybe you went to the café car, so we took a walk looking for you."

"I was just in the bathroom," I said, my voice getting higher. "He was sound asleep. I was only gone for a minute. Literally—sixty seconds, tops."

"Young lady, maybe I shouldn't butt in, but you need to keep a closer eye on your little boy. He can't watch out for himself, you know. Lots of bad things can happen to kids when you take your eyes off them, even for a second."

I nodded as he talked, but I couldn't look him in the eye.

"Now, no harm done. He's all right, see? I didn't mean to scare you, but the world's a crazy place nowadays. I wouldn't want anything to happen to either of you."

I wanted to crawl under the seats myself and stay there until morning.

"You're right," I said, because he *was* right. He was so right. "I'm sorry," I murmured. "Thank you. Thanks for everything."

"It's all right. Y'all better try and get some sleep now," he said, and he turned and walked away.

I collapsed into our seats with Wills on my lap.

"I'm such an idiot," I whispered to him. "What made me think I could take care of a little kid?"

"Kid," said Wills, yawning.

"I'm sorry," I said, rocking him. "I'm doing the best I can. I guess it's just harder than I expected."

I thought about Sandra Jean. She'd probably never be a completely decent mother. But still, she'd protected

Wills from Jake when it counted. Maybe she hadn't actually *given* my phone number to Jake. Maybe he just saw it scribbled on the magazine and helped himself.

But what about the ten grand? If she wanted Wills to be safe, why would she plant that on me and guarantee Jake coming after us?

Maybe she planted it on me figuring that, if I took Wills, the police would go looking for me. And find the money? Did Sandra Jean think the money might be evidence, too? Evidence traced to Jake? To get him arrested? And out of her life?

Cannot predict now.

Maybe Sandra Jean was trying to figure out a better life for herself, too. It was a screwy way to do it, but her life was screwed up. Maybe this was the only way she could think of. Maybe I'd been too hard on her. In her own way, maybe Sandra Jean was just doing the best she could.

Then for some reason I thought about my own mom. And dad. And for the first time in a long time, I knew that they really did love me. That they did the best they could to keep me safe in an unsafe world.

So much had happened in the past year or so—the divorce, the dangerous world, having two homes instead of one. But I still had lots more than Wills had. I'd be fine. The most important thing was to help Wills, whatever that took.

I looked down at him. "Were you really looking for your mama?"

"Mama?" said Wills, and even though it was only one word, I knew he was asking me a whole long question.

I sighed. "Wills, do you—"

I couldn't say it. I pulled him closer and kissed his head.

"It's okay," I said, rocking him. "I miss my mama too."

 TWENTY-THREE

Somehow we fell sleep. When I woke up it was sunny outside, my neck was stiff, and there was a lot of activity around us.

"Wills?" I said with a jump, suddenly remembering where I was and what had happened during the night.

"Oh, good grief." He was still on my lap, and my arms were still tight around him.

There were people everywhere, stretching and walking up and down the aisle. I could smell coffee.

I whipped out my train schedule and checked it against my watch.

It was already 8:15. That meant we were somewhere in Virginia.

"Wow," I breathed. We'd both slept like rocks. Finally.

The train stopped more frequently now, with people getting off and getting on, and the time passed quickly. Almost too quickly. Which surprised me, because on the one hand, I couldn't wait to get off that train.

But on the other hand, I could feel the pull of the vortex getting stronger. Soon we'd be facing police and reporters and parents and great aunts and—possibly—Jake. Who was going to win that battle? And on top of all that, it suddenly hit me. In a few hours, I was going to have to say goodbye to Wills.

I looked at him. He was jumping on the seat, playing I Spy out the window. He was so ready to get off the train.

Where did Miss Theresa say she lived? Brooklyn? Brooklyn wasn't that far from Farmington. But even if a miracle happened, and Wills could stay with Miss Theresa, what then? What were the chances that Wills would ever come to Farmington, Connecticut? Or that I'd be able to go to Brooklyn?

He might as well go live on the moon.

I stroked his hair and tried not to think about my heart breaking and spilling out all over the frayed and stained seats of the Amtrak Crescent.

"Busy," I said to myself. "I need to keep busy."

I rummaged through my backpack until I found one half of my hairbrush, two clean washrags, and the baby shampoo.

"Come on, Your Highness." I scooped up Wills in one arm. "We're going to make you beautiful."

"No!" he yelled. I nuzzled his cheek. He stopped kicking and started giggling.

↔ ↔ ↔

When we came out of the bathroom, we both looked halfway decent. Nothing except a real bath would make us completely decent, but at least Wills looked and smelled about 80 percent clean.

"Maybe they'll only put me in jail for ten years instead of twenty if they see that I've taken good care of you."

"Care you?" said Wills, squishing my cheeks in his hands.

I shrugged and blinked back the tears that were trying to take over. "I don't know. I wonder what they *will* do to me? Miss Theresa said she'd stand up for me. I hope that helps."

Or maybe it wouldn't matter, since I would die of a broken heart anyway.

↔ ↔ ↔

It was 9:45 AM. Twenty-seven more minutes.

What would we do if Jake was there?

I held up my hands to count who might be waiting for us at the station.

Right hand: people on my side. Mom. Miss Theresa. George the Reporter.

Left hand: people *not* on my side. Jake.

Floating in the air between my hands: Dad. The police. Maybe Sandra Jean.

That was a lot of people floating in the air. If they all floated left, Wills and I would be in big trouble.

But if I showed them my evidence, Dad and the police would have to float right. Wouldn't they?

"Well, I'm not letting go of you until I know that they're floating right," I told Wills.

He blinked up at me. "Right," he said, nodding.

I could give George the Reporter a statement to put in the newspaper: "This was not a kidnapping at all. It's been nothing more than a desperate attempt to keep a small, innocent child from falling through the cracks, which, by the way, were created by adults. I cannot make any further statements except in the presence of my attorney."

I knew I'd be too nervous to say all that. Although I was pretty sure I'd need an attorney. Wouldn't I?

Wills pulled toys out of the shopping bag one by one.

"Beeeg truck!" he said, running it along the seat. I had to pinch my arm to keep from crying.

"Let's clean out my backpack." I started by counting the stacks of bills hidden deep inside the secret compartment. The money was all there.

Then I pulled out my gossip mags.

"We don't need anyone thinking I'm an airheaded teenager," I said. "Or Mom scolding me for spending money on these again."

I tore off the corner of one magazine cover—the corner with Miss Theresa's phone number scribbled on it. I folded it over and jammed it into my jeans pocket. Then I stuffed all the magazines under the seat.

There were only a few diapers left. "That lady in Newark was right. There's a reason they put so many diapers in a package." I pulled them out of my backpack and added them to Wills' toys in the shopping bag, to give to Miss Theresa. The wipes were almost gone, but I put them in the shopping bag too.

I searched all my pockets and piled up what was left of Jake's original eight hundred dollars. I added Mom's emergency money and my Bloomingdale's money, wrapped it all in a rubber band, and tucked it deep into the bottom of the shopping bag.

I found my dead cell phone. I sort of wished I could have called Officer Martinez, to make sure he knew about my evidence, so he'd float right. But it would have to wait.

Then I wished I could call Dad.

There were so many things I needed to say to him. That I was sorry for putting him through so much, when he'd tried to help. Sorry for getting mad at him. For *being* mad at him for all these months. It wasn't all his fault. He was just doing the best he could, which I finally had to admit was pretty good most of the time.

I wanted to tell him that I loved him.

But I couldn't. We were cut off from the world for a little while longer. I put the phone in an inside, zippered pocket where it would be safe until I could give it to the police.

I found the half-empty, travel-sized bottle of baby shampoo. I unscrewed the top and inhaled deeply.

Instantly I flashed on a hot bright morning in Georgia, and a laundromat sink, and Wills' hair, fluffy and dark golden and soft in the sunlight.

I screwed the top back on tight. And then I tucked the bottle back inside my pack.

↔ ↔ ↔

The rest of the ride was a blur of cities and toys. Wills pulled out one toy after another, playing with each one for about two minutes before pulling out the next one, until all the toys were scattered on the seat. I put them all back into the bag and he started over again.

Every time we stopped, my eyes were pulled to the train schedule for the countdown to New York. With every stop my heart pounded harder and my stomach knotted tighter. I pulled Wills onto my lap and we read his books. Right in the middle of patting the bunny I realized that Wills' overalls were soggy from my sweaty hands holding him so tight.

"Stop it!" I said to myself.

"What?" said Wills.

"No, not you, buddy," I said. "I'm just reminding myself why we did this in the first place. It was to protect you. To keep you from falling through the cracks. And the fight's not over yet. I have to stay focused here."

"Here!" said Wills, bouncing on my lap.

And then, almost before I knew it, we were practically there. Penn Station was the next stop.

I swallowed hard and rubbed my eyes dry. I ran the brush through William's hair one last time and packed all his toys into the shopping bag.

Then I pulled him onto my lap and we sang.

You are my sunshine
My only sunshine
You make me happy
When skies are gray.
You'll never know, dear
How much I love you.
Please don't take my sunshine away.

And suddenly, we were there.

Pulling into Penn Station.

Into the center of the vortex.

TWENTY-FOUR

"Okay now," I said when the train went underground for the home stretch. He looked at me with those bottomless eyes and I had to blink hard.

"I think it might be kind of crazy once we get off the train. There might be lots of policemen. *He* might be there. But Miss Theresa will be there for sure. Do you want to go outside and see Tee?"

"Tee," he said, smiling big.

I smiled back at him. "I bet she can't wait to see you, either."

And me? Would I ever see Wills again after today?
Outlook not so good.

"Wills, look at me. If I tell you something—something very important—do you think you could remember it for a long time?"

"Down," he said. "Tee?"

"I know, but the train hasn't stopped yet. Listen to me, please, Wills?"

He sat still and looked up at me, waiting. I tried to commit every hair and eyelash to memory. "I want you to know that—"

The train lurched and we almost fell off the seat. Wills giggled. I squeezed him tight and fell backward into the seat with him in my arms. I whispered into his ear.

"I just love you, that's all. I promise to be strong for you. I promise not to cry, and I promise on my life to give you to nobody but Tee. And no matter what happens, I'll never, ever let you fall through the cracks."

Wills sat up and looked me square in the eye, like maybe he'd actually stored all my words into his brain forever.

Then he squished my cheeks in his hands and kissed my puckered lips. "Outside?" he said. "Tee?"

I bit my lip and smiled.

"Yep. We're going outside to see Tee."

I saw Mom and Dad on the platform before the train even stopped. They must have seen us too, because they turned and ran to keep up with us.

The brakes squealed until I thought my eardrums

would burst. I covered William's ears with my hands. Then the doors all hissed open, and everything was quiet.

I stood up and scanned the crowd through the windows, looking for Jake and at the same time trying to figure out which face might be Miss Theresa's. My knees shook and I had to sit down again.

"Stop it, Victoria," I told myself. "You made Wills a promise and you have to keep it. You didn't put him through all this just to flake out now. You have to be strong."

I forced myself to wait until everyone else was off the train and the platform wasn't so crowded.

I pointed out the window. "Do you see Tee out there anywhere?"

"Tee?" he said, without bothering to look for her. He wiggled and bounced in my arms. "Outside?"

"I guess this is it." I took a deep breath. "The inevitable. Here we go."

I stood up. I gathered up bags and backpack and baby. Somehow I moved my feet until we were standing at the top of the steps, in the open door of the train.

There were four people standing on the platform below our door. Mom and Dad were there, all out of breath and red in the face from running. And a policeman—just one. And a very young woman in a very ugly suit.

No one else.

The policeman seemed kind of old for a cop, and tired, with bags under his eyes.

The ugly suit lady whispered something into his ear while she looked at us out of the corner of her eye.

The policeman stepped forward and put one foot on the bottom step.

"Victoria, I'm Officer Martinez. And this is Miss Campbell," he said, tipping his head toward the ugly suit lady. "She's a social worker from the Office of Children and Family Services." He held his arms out. "Why don't you hand Danny down to me."

And Mom and Dad came up behind him, nodding, and they all started talking at once, so I couldn't understand a word any of them was saying.

I took a step back, and bumped into something.

Or someone. It was the conductor with the shiny belt buckle.

"Hey, kiddo," he said.

"Victoria," said Officer Martinez from the platform. "Detective Carlson can help you down."

"Detective—?" I stared at him. "You're not a conductor?"

Detective Carlson shook his head and shrugged. "Amtrak police."

Then it all made sense. "That's why you knew Wills was on the seat when you punched my ticket. You knew the whole time?"

He nodded. "NYPD said you called your dad and informed him of your plans. Then they called us."

Now it was my turn to nod. But then I wondered. "You didn't ask for my ID or anything, though . . . "

Detective Carlson reached into his breast pocket and pulled out a piece of paper.

It was grainy, in black and white. But there was no mistaking my face in the surveillance photo.

Then I looked up at him, and I whispered, "Thanks for letting us come home."

"You're welcome," said Detective Carlson. "It's time to go now, though."

Officer Martinez was standing at the bottom of the steps, reaching up for Wills.

"Wait a minute," I said. "Where's George? Where's Miss Theresa?"

"Who?" asked Mom. "Honey, it's just us. Come down now. It's all over."

I shook my head. "No, it's not. I need Miss Theresa. She said she'd be here. Where is she?"

"Victoria," said Dad. He had stubble on his face and his clothes were wrinkled. "Please, honey. Don't make this any harder. Give the baby to Officer Martinez."

My knees were shaking again, until I thought that any second Wills and I would both tumble down the steps. So many people, holding their arms out, nodding, telling me what to do.

And then I broke my first promise to Wills. My eyes filled with tears and I had to grab the door because everything was so blurry.

"She has to be here," I said, but my throat was tight and I knew they couldn't hear me. "She said she'd be here. She promised."

I scanned the platform desperately, but there was no one else. Only Mom and Dad and Officer Martinez and

Miss Ugly Suit. No one else stopped, or even seemed to notice what was going on.

My knees gave out and I sat down right on the top step with my face buried in Wills' neck. All I could hear was his voice, saying over and over, "Tee? Tee?"

And then I felt a pair of big hands. Pulling my arms apart.

"Come on, now, Danny. I won't hurt you." It was Officer Martinez.

Wills started to cry, and he wrapped his arms tight around my neck and his legs around my ribs.

But the hands were strong and sturdy and gentle and cruel. They pried my arms open. The voice spoke softly to Wills. The tired face smiled at him. Wills cried and I cried, but the policeman said, "Don't worry, now. Everything is going to be just fine."

And suddenly, I had broken my second promise.

Officer Martinez carried Wills down the steps to the platform and handed him to Miss Ugly Suit. From behind me, Officer Carlson touched my elbow and said softly, "Victoria, it's over now. It's time to go."

And then I heard Wills' voice. It sounded so far away. "Sunshine?"

I could hardly bear to look at him. He was crying and wiggling in Miss Ugly Suit's arms, and reaching toward me. She had trouble keeping her grip on him.

"No!" I shouted, practically jumping down the steps onto the platform. Miss Ugly Suit took a step back in surprise. I reached for Wills, and he wiggled even harder.

"Please!" I begged. "I can't leave him. I promised him . . . ."

"Victoria," Officer Martinez said. "It's out of your hands now."

And all of a sudden I knew he was right.

It *was* over.

And I had lost.

I'd failed Wills miserably and I had no one to stand up for me or write my story in the newspaper and everything had gone so completely wrong. I covered my face with my hands. I couldn't bear to look at Wills.

"Victoria?" said a soft voice.

"Mom," I sobbed, falling into her arms. "She's not here. Why isn't she here?"

"Who, honey? Who are you expecting?"

But I couldn't even get the words out any more.

Then Wills squealed, "Tee! Tee!"

Someone was hurrying toward us with her arms out.

"Tee!" he squealed, and he practically threw himself out of Miss Ugly Suit's arms. "Tee!"

And Miss Theresa caught him, and they held each other so tight I thought no one would ever be able to pull them apart.

"Danny, my Danny! Oh, my baby boy!" she said, laughing and crying and kissing him and rocking him. "You look so wonderful. So wonderful!" And she kissed him and kissed him and kissed him.

Miss Ugly Suit stood there with her mouth open. Mom and Dad were totally confused. Officer Martinez put his hands on his hips and shook his head.

"Where is she?" Miss Theresa said to Wills. And she looked right at me. I swallowed hard.

"Victoria?"

"Yes, ma'am." I would have known it was her even without Wills to tell me. She had those same bottomless eyes.

"Let me see you, dear." She stepped over to me and took my hand. And even though she was about half my size, I thought she would break a bone in one of my fingers.

"Thank you for keeping your word, Victoria. Thank you for taking such good care of Danny." She looked at him again, smiling. "I can tell he's been in good hands."

"May I quote you on that, ma'am?" said a voice.

I looked up to see a man standing there, out of breath and holding a little tape recorder in one hand and business cards in the other. He passed out cards to the police officers, Miss Ugly Suit, Dad, and Miss Theresa. "George Silva, ladies and gentlemen. *New York Times*." Then he looked at me and shrugged.

"Sorry," he said. "Damn Seventh Avenue traffic."

I looked back at Miss Theresa, and at Wills, who was smiling so big and kissing his Tee all over her face.

"Miss Theresa, I'm—thanks for coming." I held out the shopping bag full of toys and diapers, and she took it.

"It's all right, darlin'. Everything will be all right." And she turneds and said, "Officers? I need to have a word with you."

The rest was a blur. Miss Theresa was talking to Officer Martinez. George the reporter was holding up the tape recorder and Miss Ugly Suit was shaking her head and telling him something, and then Mom and Dad both swamped me and started talking, and I couldn't really hear what anyone was saying. All I heard were bits and pieces floating from all their mouths, all jumbled together... "so glad you're home" ... "you can't possibly press charges" ... "what happened to your hair?" ... "no one told me about an aunt" ... "I have a source that says..."

"Dad—" I started.

"Honey, this has all been my fault, for not being there to meet your train in the first place. I haven't been there for you much at all, and that's not right."

We looked at each other for a long minute. Then I threw my arms around him. "I'm sorry too, Dad," I whispered. And he squeezed me tight.

After a while, everyone stopped talking. Officer Martinez turned to me. Mom put her arm around my shoulders.

"Victoria, I'm sure you realize that there's a lot of legal business that needs to be worked out," said Officer Martinez. "It looks like you have a couple of advocates here, and Danny has a blood relative who can act as temporary guardian. That's all very good news. But you'll have to come with me so we can start figuring things out. Your parents will come too."

"Where's Jake?"

"Your dad said you have proof of possible illegal activity on Jake's part?"

I handed him my backpack. "It's in here. And he's not Danny's father."

Officer Martinez took my pack and nodded. "There've

been more than a few inconsistencies in his story the past couple of days. They're talking to him down at the station. We need to head over there too. But don't worry, he won't see you."

"Are you going to handcuff me?" I asked.

He smiled his tired smile. "Do I need to?"

I shook my head.

Miss Theresa came over to us again. "Victoria, try not to worry. It'll be all right. I promise."

Then I heard another voice that made my heart jump all over again.

"Sunshine?"

Everyone stopped talking and looked at Wills.

I stepped over to him and took his hand. It was soft and warm, and it squeezed my fingers.

"Hi, buddy," I said to him softly.

He smiled at me, with his pretty little white teeth and his bottomless, Magic Eight Ball eyes. Then he pulled his hand out of mine, held it up, and opened and closed his fist.

"'Bye, Sunshine," he said. "'Bye!"

He wrapped his skinny little arms around Miss Theresa's head and pressed his cheek against hers.

And then he was gone.

 TWENTY-FIVE

If you cross state lines, kidnapping is a federal crime. Grand juries, the FBI. Sort of like the big leagues of the criminal justice system.

But, if the kidnap-ee wasn't harmed, or if you didn't demand a monetary ransom, the Feds can bump you down to state jurisdiction, because it's also a state crime. *And* it's a felony, Class A-1, in the first degree, which means they're required by law to lock you up for at least a year and you'll have a criminal record for the rest of your life. Kiss your future good-bye, young lady.

However. If you happen to be a kidnapper who's younger than sixteen, forget all of the above and start over. Because if your attorney can prove that it's "in the best interests of justice," you'll get sent to Family Court instead, where you're not technically a "criminal," you're a "juvenile offender," or in other words just plain "delinquent." So, even though you committed the aforementioned Class A-1 first degree felony kidnapping, if you're just a kid yourself, and if the judge feels like it, he can decide it's better to rehabilitate you than to punish you. It's all a matter of jurisdiction. Get it?

But wait. Let's not forget about "compelling circumstances." There are compelling circumstances if the kidnapper (i.e., *me*) had reason to fear for the victim's (i.e., *Wills'*) safety. Compelling circumstances could result in a motion to dismiss, which means the judge—if he feels like it—could decide that a crime was never even committed in the first place. In other words, the "this whole thing was a huge misunderstanding so let's forget it ever happened" defense.

We were pinning our hopes on the motion to dismiss.

And, no matter how long it takes, under *no* circumstances is Miss Kidnapper allowed to have any contact What So Ever with The Kidnap-ee, or his great-aunt. Not even a phone call. That would be considered harassment. Potential witness tampering, even. A big fat huge no-no. I'm sorry, but it just isn't done.

So on top of everything else—on top of watching the circles under your parents' eyes getting darker by the week; seeing them miss day after day of work and slowly be buried under legal bills; after spending hours in lawyers' offices; and after being the topic of reams of senseless legal and legislative blathering—you have to be a good girl and politely ignore the fact that you have no idea what happened to Wills, or to Sandra Jean, or to Jake for that matter, and no one on earth is willing or able to help you find out. "I'm sorry, Victoria," said my overpriced lawyer in the Brooks Brothers suit. "We're just not a party to that information."

There really should be stricter rules for the use of the word *party*.

So I had to depend on George.

Every morning I grabbed the Metro section out of the *Times* to see if there was any news.

At first it was on Page One:

Penn Station Kidnapping: Abduction or Abandonment?

It was a whole big article about how the anonymous minor who took the anonymous toddler argued that she was trying to protect an abandoned, possibly abused child.

Good ol' George.

But nothing in the paper on the fate of the abandoned/abducted toddler, good or bad.

The next day came the article that opened the can of worms at the Office of Children and Family Services. It turned out they already had a file on Wills, just like Miss Theresa had said. But it had been closed months ago.

Over the course of the next few weeks, George wrote about a shake-up of the whole Family Services department that started over Wills' prematurely closed file. By the end of the summer, five social workers were fired and the director of the department quit. Which was all very well and good. It was an effort to seal the cracks. I hoped it would work, and that other kids, besides Wills, would somehow benefit because of it. When Wills and I were running, it never occurred to me that we were making a statement for lots of kids. But I guess we were, and I have to say I feel good about that, or at least hopeful. The world is a dangerous place. Every kid needs a safe home. Every kid deserves to be loved. Is that so much to ask?

As the days went by, the articles got shorter and shorter. They mostly focused on the Office of Children and Family Services. Bureaucracies and politicians and taxpayer dollars.

Whatever.

I only wanted to know one thing: What about Wills?

Then one day late in August, when I was getting ready to head back to Connecticut to start school (and commute back to the city for my court appearances), I saw it, in the last paragraph of a short article in the back of the Metro section:

Meanwhile, the child whose case sparked the state's investigation has passed a personal milestone. Two separate petitions for permanent custody have been filed in Family Court, one of which was granted and one denied. The party whose petition was denied is expected to appeal the decision.

As Mom and I rode back to Hartford on the train, I pulled the crumpled piece of newspaper out of my pocket and read that paragraph over and over again, trying to fill in the blanks. The two separate petitions had to be Miss Theresa and Sandra Jean. But whose petition was granted, and whose was denied?

They must have granted custody to Miss Theresa. It was the only reasonable choice. They had plenty of evidence that Sandra Jean was an unfit mother.

Didn't they?

But she'd protected Wills from Jake, that first day in Penn Station. She was his mother, and she loved him. And something inside me told me that Wills loved her, too. That Wills needed his mother, no matter how imperfect she was. Maybe that's what the judge thought, too. Maybe he granted custody to Sandra Jean after all.

But it wasn't over yet, because whoever was denied custody wasn't happy about it. It gave me even more reason to hope—and even more reason to worry, and wonder.

Outside my window, the city faded to suburbs and the suburbs faded to fields. I tried to convince myself that the ending I wanted for Wills would somehow come true. But every time I decided I was convinced, those words poked at me: *She's his mother.*

And until my own case was over, I couldn't know for sure. I wasn't a party to that information.

I did have one piece of information that no one else had. I didn't really need the torn scrap of magazine cover, because the number was permanently imprinted on my brain. But I pulled the paper out of my pocket anyway, carefully smoothed it flat, and looked at it. I ran my finger along its torn edge, and I touched it to my nose, hoping it might still hold a vague aroma of baby shampoo.

But it just smelled like paper.

The thing is, it's easy to make promises. It can be a lot harder to keep them.

But loving someone isn't only making promises you *know* you can keep. That's just playing it safe. Where's the moral fiber in that? Loving someone is making promises you *want* to keep with all your heart, and then doing everything you can to make it happen, even if you fail sometimes. But the point is to try, because that's how you stretch yourself and learn you can do more than you thought you could. And maybe next time, you'll stretch a little farther.

I decided that from now on, I'd go easier on Mom and Dad, because even though they couldn't always keep their promises, they stretched. I decided we could all stretch together, and maybe somehow we'd meet in the middle.

I carefully folded the scrap of paper and put it back in my pocket. For now, I wouldn't call, and I wouldn't harass, and I wouldn't tamper. I would wait, and I would wish and hope and pray for the only ending that could possibly be. But I promised myself that one day, when it was finally allowed, I'd dial that number, and then I'd know for sure.

And that was a promise I knew I'd keep.

The End

About the Author

Growing up in Wisconsin, Stacy DeKeyser spent her summers at the library, reading and dreaming about faraway places. Since then, she has traveled to twenty-seven states and six foreign countries. Now she lives in Connecticut and frequently takes the train to New York City. This is her first novel. Visit her online at www.stacydekeyser.com.